Revolt on Alpha C

By ROBERT SILVERBERG

Illustrated by William Meyerriecks

SCHOLASTIC  BOOK SERVICES

Published by Scholastic Book Services, a division
of Scholastic Magazines, Inc., New York, N.Y.

FOR MY PARENTS

This book is sold subject to the condition that it shall not be resold,
lent, or otherwise circulated in any binding or cover other than
that in which it is published—unless prior written permission has
been obtained from the publisher—and without a similar condition,
including this condition, being imposed on the subsequent purchaser.

Copyright 1955 by Robert Silverberg. Copyright © 1959 by TAB
Books, Inc. This edition is published by Scholastic Book
Services, a division of Scholastic Magazines, Inc., by arrange-
ment with Thomas Y. Crowell Company.

7th printing.............January 1969

Printed in the U.S.A.

CHAPTER 1

THE STOPOVER at Pluto was brief, but for Larry Stark it seemed to be much too long. The *Carden* and its crew had spent a week on the cold, small planet at the outermost edge of the solar system, making the necessary change-over to overdrive. This was the second stop on the journey that would take him to the fourth planet of the star Alpha Centauri, four and a half light-years away.

The conversion of the *Carden* for interstellar travel was necessary if they wanted to cross that gulf of space in less than a decade. Standard drive was limited to use within the solar system, and it operated at a comparatively slow maximum speed of 100,000 miles per second. The overdrive installed on Pluto would enable the *Carden* to travel the trillions of miles to

Alpha C in a little over two weeks; without the drive the trip would take years.

Larry was impatient to get on to Alpha C. The stop at Mars had been made in order to pick up Harl Ellison, like Larry a newly graduated cadet of the Space Patrol Academy. They were making their Final Cruise— the traditional post-graduation space cruise, at the end of which they would be awarded their commissions as officers of the Patrol.

Most of the Cruises had been to points within the solar system. But Larry, and Harl, who had studied at the Martian branch of the Academy, and Heitor van Haaren and three other Earth Academy cadets, had been chosen to go on the first Interstellar Cruise in Academy history. They were on their way to the primitive fourth planet of Alpha Centauri, where four small Earth colonies struggled for existence amid a prehistoric environment.

Larry had secretly hoped that his father, Commander Stark of the Space Patrol, would use his influence to get him assigned to the coveted Interstellar Cruise. But Larry had not dared mention the matter, knowing that his father's code of honor would allow no such thing, and had earned his way abroad by finishing first in his class at the Academy. His father had been tremendously proud; Larry came from a long line of Space Patrol commanders, and his father was determined that his son would keep up the tradition. It was hard to tell which one was more happy when the notification came that Larry had been chosen for the Cruise.

The trip to Mars had been full of excitement, but the novelty of life in space lost some of its glitter during the nine-day journey to Pluto for the change-over to overdrive. Still, ahead of him lay Alpha C IV, a young world peopled by giant dinosaurs, and the delay on Pluto nearly exhausted Larry's patience.

At last the overhauling of the *Carden* was finished and he could say good-by to the bleak, snow-covered world. The crew of the *Carden* made quick farewells to the colonists who lived under the dome on Pluto and trotted back across the snow to the ship to await blastoff.

Larry stared out the port while stowing his things for blastoff. He looked at the white blanket of snow, broken here and there by jagged splinters of rock towering high above, and at the black sky with the sun a bright dash of light, hard and brilliant without any appearance of warmth. This was the sun, Larry knew, as it appeared from the uttermost depths of its realm.

He compared the Plutonian landscape with the view of Mars as he recalled it from the brief glimpse he had had. Mars was starkly monotonous, without trees, all bleak and barren for vast distances, a brick-red desert with scraggly patches of green. Neither Mars nor Pluto was suitable for human life except under the protection of a dome. But ahead of him was Alpha Centauri IV, where the air was fresh and warm and the forests thrived with growing things.

Larry cushioned himself in his acceleration cradle and braced against the shock of blastoff, as the *Carden* escaped from Pluto's grip. The great roar of the jets filled the cabin and an invisible fist bashed Larry down against the cradle. The *Carden* sprang up away from Pluto, stood for a moment on a fiery tail, and then headed outward to the stars.

Now the long haul started, the fifteen-day trip from Pluto to Earth's nearest stellar neighbor.

Actually Alpha Centauri was not the closest star;

3

Proxima Centauri, an insignificant star with no planets, was slightly closer to Earth. But around Alpha C there whirled eleven planets, of which one—the fourth from the sun—was inhabitable by human beings. A colony had been planted there some 125 years before, and one on a planet of the bright star Sirius, about twice as far from Earth as Alpha C.

In the twentieth century the great Einstein had pointed out that it was impossible for a moving body to exceed the speed of light, 186,000 miles per second. The Lorentz-Fitzgerald equations showed the strange effects which would take place when a body approached the speed of light.

But "impossible" is a word not found in the vocabulary of most scientists.

The Huxley discovery of 2183 gave man the path to the stars. Until then, faster-than-light travel was impossible. And, with traveling speeds limited to the velocity of light, it would take almost five years to make the trip to Alpha C; nine years, round-trip.

Huxley's discovery was a method of warping space, a new drive principle called "overdrive."

Larry's main duty aboard ship was to serve as radio operator, the specialty which he had chosen while in the Academy. Once a day he transmitted the ship's log, dictated by grizzle-haired, iron-faced Captain Reinhardt, a stern old spaceman who reminded Larry of his father and whom he had once nearly addressed as "Dad" in an absent-minded moment.

Larry would transmit the log regularly to the Space Bureau, which required daily contact with all ships in space. The rest of his working day was devoted to taking care of the radio instruments and picking up occasional messages beamed to the ship.

4

His schedule allowed him frequent free hours which he usually spent in his cabin, along with Harl Ellison, the Martian cadet he bunked with. Ellison was short, a head shorter than Larry, broad-shouldered, barrel-chested, and sturdy. Like all Martians he was heavily tanned.

"We enter overdrive sometime tomorrow," Larry said as he entered the cabin. "Reinhardt entered it in today's log."

"Quiet!" Harl said. "If I know anything about Earthmen this whole ship's probably wired for sound, and you know you're not supposed to be telling me what's in the log." Harl's voice was deep and booming, a low growl emanating from somewhere in his huge chest.

Larry smiled and sprawled out on his berth. "I doubt it," he said. "Why would they want to wire us for sound? Don't they trust us?"

Harl leaned back and closed the book he had been studying. "I know Earthmen," he repeated. "They're probably listening to us right now."

There was a knock on the door of the cabin. Harl and Larry exchanged glances.

"Come in," Larry called.

The door opened and Olcott, the pilot, a veteran spaceman, entered.

"I got your note," he said. "What did you want to talk to me about, Larry?"

"It's this: I've been looking through the textbooks, and none of them answers a question I'm puzzled about. Why does overdrive work?"

Olcott chuckled and sat down. "Why? Why does it work? No one knows that, Larry—not even old Huxley himself. No one knows exactly how electricity works, either, or magnetism, but we manage to control them."

"I thought maybe you could help me out, Olcott.

5

They don't teach us too much about overdrive at the Academy."

Harl nodded. "They sort of passed over it at the Martian Academy too, Larry. They seemed uneasy."

"It's pretty simple," Olcott said. "We don't know why it works, but we know how it works. It's a spacewarp. Look: it folds space over on itself, making sort of an accordion pleat where we go through."

He picked up a sheet of paper on which Larry had been doing some equations. "Here. Imagine space as this piece of paper. You have to travel from one side of the paper to the other, and the distance is four inches. Got the picture?"

"Yes, but space isn't flat—"

"Never mind that for a moment," Olcott put in. "Just follow me. Now, instead of making this journey all the way across the flat surface, you find some way of folding up the edges so where you are and where you want to be are right next to each other. Then you just cross over, and you've made your trip of four inches without moving more than a couple of millimeters.

"So what the Huxley Drive does is to go outside the normal three dimensions—to go above them, in a way—and cause that folding effect. Then we just cross from one edge to the other, and we've made our journey in hardly any time at all."

Olcott stood up as if to leave. "By the way, we enter overdrive tomorrow, in case you haven't heard. I suppose it's all right to tell you."

"Why don't we ever use overdrive within the solar system?" Larry asked.

Harl suppressed a laugh. "And you're number one in the Earth Academy? Use your head, Larry—it's like using an H-Bomb to kill a rabbit, to use the Huxley Drive to go from Earth to Mars."

"Harl's right," Olcott said. "It's not very precise. It's hard to pin your distances down to a few million miles. If you tried to go from Earth to Mars, more likely than not you'd end up near Jupiter, or maybe you'd come out of overdrive right inside Mars itself—and that would destroy the whole planet. So overdrive is never used within the system."

"That's why we stop off at Pluto before heading out, eh?"

"That's it. Pluto is the last outpost of the system, and then there's nothing but space for four light-years. So all outbound ships stop off there and have their drive mechanisms changed; the standard one is removed and a Huxley Drive installed. Then we stop back there on the return trip."

Larry nodded. "Does space look any different in overdrive?"

"I'm afraid not. It's not very strange. You wouldn't be able to see anything, but there's nothing to see anyway. It's empty out there; empty and black and cold. It's space, Larry, and space is a lonely thing."

"I know," Larry said, looking hard at the old spaceman's tired face. "I know."

The final leg of the journey, that to Alpha C, was scheduled to last fifteen days. Of that time, some six days were being used to get clear of Pluto, and seven days would be used to coast into Alpha C IV. The remaining two days would be spent in overdrive, and in those days they would cover four light-years, or twenty-five million million miles. The *Carden* would range out through the vast emptiness and come out of overdrive a few million miles from its destination.

7

Larry was fast learning to appreciate the great loneliness of the spacemen. A spaceship was a world in
itself, a tiny metal world floating between the stars.
There was no corner candy store, no evening paper,
no game of ball in the street.

There were long hours of staring at the velvet
blackness of space, and hours of study, and hours of
work. And in the evening, the same group would
gather all the time. A spaceship is a small world, with
five or ten or a dozen people, or maybe twenty or
thirty. But no more. Never any strangers, never anyone
new moving into the block. A small, quiet, self-con-
tained, self-sufficient world.

And the men of space, Larry found, those gods in
gray uniforms, they felt the loneliness. But it was part
of them; no, it *was* them. Space filtered in and mingled
with the calcium in their bones.

Space meant waiting. Larry discovered that traveling in space meant long periods in the ship, broken
by a few moments on this world, a few hours on that.
He had been on Mars a day, had seen that broken
and twisted half-dead world, and then had pulled up
stakes again. Then it was Pluto, a weird world of
frozen fields, and then back to space again.

And now the long haul, the big trip. To the next
star.

Out ahead was Alpha C. Larry stood staring out into
the long night of space as if to search for the planet
that lay somewhere ahead.

It was July 7, six days out from Pluto. The visiphone
crackled to life and the announcement filled the ship.

*Prepare for overdrive. We enter overdrive in ten sec-
onds.*

Larry and Harl hastily strapped themselves into their

acceleration cradles, not knowing any other way of preparaing for overdrive. *Nine. Eight.*

The voice pounded out the seconds over the visiphone. *Seven. Six. Five.*

"Empty out there. Empty and black and cold," Olcott had said. Larry wondered what would happen to the ship as it shifted to overdrive. *Four. Three.*

Larry looked across the cabin at Harl. They grinned. Larry felt the excitement pounding in him, just as it had the first time he had blasted off from Earth. Once again he was moving into the Unknown.

Two. One.

Swiftly there came a twist and a squeak and the ship seemed to spin around Larry's head for a minute. Then all grew still.

The *Carden* had erupted into overdrive.

CHAPTER 2

OVERDRIVE PROVED to be nothing unusual after the first twisting shock of conversion, and life proceeded as usual aboard the *Carden*.

The only difference, so far as Larry was concerned, was that during overdrive it was impossible to use the radio equipment, and so he was on relief for the two days the *Carden* would spend on the Huxley Drive. As soon as he found this out, he headed for the rear jet section, where huge O'Hare would be sitting, strumming his electronic guitar and bellowing out the songs of space.

O'Hare was a tubemonkey, a member of that lower class of spacemen who tended the jets, did menial work, and rarely came forward to join in the society of the ship. He was an immense red-haired man with

10

intense blue eyes and a powerful bass voice, who spent most of his free time playing his intricate electronic guitar and singing. He had become friendly with Larry before blastoff from Earth, and the two had remained close friends despite the silent disapproval of some of the officers, who did not like cadets mingling with tubemonkeys.

"I've got two days off," Larry told Harl. "Radio won't be able to make contact with anyone till we're out of overdrive. I'm heading back to the jets."

Harl, bent over a textbook, merely nodded, and Larry went out. He strode down the familiar corridor and into the lead-walled jet section, where he saw O'Hare and his two assistants carrying things from wall to wall far at the other side of the jet chamber.

"Pat!" Larry called. The big Irishman put down whatever he had been carrying and came over.

"Ho, laddy! You draw a blank during overdrive, don't you? It's a soft life you radiomen lead." The giant was stripped to the waist and sweating. "We were just stowing some fuel pellets when you showed up." He lifted his hand to his mouth as a megaphone and yelled to the two men still working. "Boggs! Grennell! Knock off and come over here."

They came. They were both big, husky men—though not as big as O'Hare. They greeted Larry curtly.

Grennell was a squat, broad-shouldered fellow with sharp features and an ugly red scar on one cheek. Boggs was tall, with close-cropped hair and thick, vein-corded forearms.

O'Hare lowered himself to the floor and propped himself up against the lead-lined wall.

"How come Reinhardt hasn't reassigned you for these two days?" O'Hare asked. "He hates to waste a man."

11

"I'll say," Grennell agreed. "He'll work you till you drop."

Larry frowned. The jetmen were forever grumbling about the captain. This was one thing he found hard to take; his training all through life, from his father and later at the Academy, taught him to respect his officers.

"Maybe he just forgot about me. He—"

But O'Hare wasn't listening. He was rippling his hand, his great veined hand, over the controls of the guitar. A few chords drifted out. He looked off into the distance and began to sing, mournfully, in his resonant basso.

> Oh, Mars is dry and bare of life—
> Gone the race of Mars.
> Peace on the world of the god of strife—
> Gone the race of Mars.

Grennell picked up the melody there. His voice was deep and hard, but underneath was the mixture of melodiousness and rough tenderness which creeps into the voices of all spacemen. Grennell sang the plaintive minor refrain.

> The towers stand in the desert—
> Bone-dry and dusty, all.
> The race that built them also's dust,
> Faces to the wall.

The visiphone clicked.

All hands to quarters, came the announcement.

Larry looked around uneasily. He knew he had to get back to his cabin; being out against orders would get him in trouble. The first rule, when the back-to-quarters signal was given, was to get back to quarters.

But none of the tubemonkeys were moving, none showed the slightest sign of having heard the announcement, and Larry decided to follow their example and ignore the warning. There was bound to be a second call for back-to-quarters, and he could leave then. He knew how these men felt about Captain Reinhardt's authority, and he did not want to displease them by seeming too easily ordered around.

"That's pretty gloomy music," Boggs said, making one of his rare contributions to the conversation.

O'Hare gave no answer, but began strumming harder and faster, and wild chords leaped from the instrument. He threw his head back and roared.

> The men of space are a hardy race,
> They're built of fire and stone
> They roam the stars and know no bars
> In space they find their home.

It was the familiar, hundred-versed ballad that was the unofficial anthem of the spacemen. Larry joined the chorus in his clear baritone, and Boggs and Grennell followed.

> Heigh-ho! Hear the jets!
> Feel them blast, feel them rip, heigh-ho!
> Feel them blast!
> Feel them rip!
> Oh, heigh-ho!

O'Hare took up the solo again.

> Oh, I was born on Alpha C
> Among the dinosaurs.
> I'm ten feet high and bold and free—

13

But the song was interrupted. The visiphone crackled to life and the announcement filled the jet section.

All hands back to quarters! Emergency! Emergency!

In the middle of a note O'Hare put down the guitar, leaped up, and ran to his jets; Boggs and Grennell did likewise. Larry suddenly realized he should have been in his cabin long ago, and headed for the corridor. He began to race down the hall, aware that he had broken a regulation.

There came an abrupt twist and there was the shock of change-over as the *Carden* burst out of overdrive. Larry grew dizzy and sank to his knees. The corridor wall was racing around his head, coming closer and closer each time around. An immense bulkhead loomed up and grazed past his head.

Larry fell flat, hardly conscious of what was happening, and began to crawl along the floor toward his cabin. Somewhere in the back of his mind he wondered what his father, resplendent in the uniform of a commander in the Space Patrol, would think if he saw his son creeping along the floor because he had disobeyed an instruction. Then the ship gave another lurch and he sank into unconsciousness.

CHAPTER 3

LARRY FELT a stinging slap against his cheek.
He waved his arm vaguely, trying to drive away his
attacker, and slowly returned to consciousness.

"Stop that," he mumbled, as another slap brought
him further awake. He looked up to see O'Hare standing over him, preparing to bring down his hand once
again.

"Never mind. I'm awake," he said, hastily scram-
bling to his feet and rubbing the side of his face.
"What happened? Why are we back in regular drive?"

"I don't know, laddy," O'Hare said. He looked worried. "Reinhardt's called a general meeting in the Central Room to discuss the situation, and we're late."

"I was on my way back when we shifted over," Larry
said as they hurried down the corridor to the Central

15

Room. "The twist caught me and I must have banged my head on a bulkhead."

He felt a sudden twinge of pain from the bruise on his head, reminding him of his carelessness in not returning to his cabin when the order came. Dad wouldn't like this at all, not at all, he thought, remembering the way the sunlight glinted from the gold braid on his father's uniform.

They entered the Central Room, O'Hare first, Larry behind. The entire crew was ringed around the room, with Captain Reinhardt standing stiff and erect in the middle. He looked sternly at the two latecomers.

"Now that the complete crew is here, we can begin. You two may file written excuses for your lateness."

They nodded. The veteran captain seemed to stare hard at Larry, in just the way his father would, and Larry felt like hiding behind O'Hare. The big tube-monkey met the captain's stare impassively.

"Now. Here's what happened." Captain Reinhardt spoke in short, hard, staccato bursts of sound. "There's something in the jets. Some kind of obstruction. Could be anything—meteor, dirt accumulation, anything. Probably just a speck of dust that floated in and managed the million-to-one. Something has disturbed the balances of our drive mechanism and shut off the overdrive."

He looked around at the crew. "If we don't get our drive fixed, it's going to take us four years to reach Alpha C—sometime in 2367. And 2367's a long time. We only have food for four weeks, not four years.

"We can only reach the mechanism from outside the ship. O'Hare, it's your department, so you're going outside to clear it up. Get yourself into a spacesuit and start moving."

O'Hare said nothing, but saluted and left to get into

his spacesuit. Larry watched his departure. Going out into space was risky—standing there on the skin of the ship, with the cold of space held away by the thin protection of the spacesuit—but it was absolutely necessary that O'Hare go outside. If the drive stayed off, they would run out of food years before they reached Alpha C. And finding a ship in space was harder than looking for a needle in a haystack, so there was little chance of a rescue.

"It violates space rules to send a man outside alone," Captain Reinhardt said. "Cadet Stark, your lateness to this meeting is construed as volunteering to accompany O'Hare. Get a suit on and join him."

Larry stared blankly for just a moment, but his control reasserted itself almost immediately. He saluted smartly and left, without saying a word.

So this was space at first hand, Larry thought as he climbed through the airlock. His suit and helmet was a closed system, ventilated, protected from the biting cold of space. His one contact with humanity was the radio in his helmet. In one space-gloved hand he held a small gun; another was clamped to his suit at the hip. On his feet were magnetic shoes.

O'Hare was already out there, moving slowly along the ship to the jet section. Larry followed, carefully placing his feet on the steel walking tracks. The magnet clicked and he knew he was held fast. He switched on his helmet-radio with a movement of his chin.

"Pat! Wait for me."

O'Hare twisted around till he could see the face in the space helmet.

"Larry! You too?"

"Reinhardt sent me. Thought you'd get lonesome."

O'Hare's curses were vivid. "He's thought nothing

17

of sending me out here alone before. It's just that he wanted to give you a bad time of it for coming late to his useless meeting." O'Hare turned and continued moving. "But what would you expect from him? Or any Patrol officer? They're all alike—steel bellies."

He gestured with his hand. "Let's go, laddy. You're safe enough out here. Let's get this over with. I'd like to flay that captain's duralumin hide!"

"Don't talk like that, Pat," Larry said. "He *is* the captain, whether you like him or not."

"Sorry, lad. I forget you're from the Academy. But you'll learn, someday, I hope. Come on—let's move."

Larry puzzled over what O'Hare had said—"you'll learn, someday." What would he learn? Not to obey the captain? Impossible. The captain *had* to be obeyed; otherwise how would society stay preserved? If every man were his own captain there would never be any tubemonkeys.

He looked around at his view. Space was naked before him. The ship seemed not to move at all; it hung motionless, floating in the void. All around there was blackness, broken by dots of light scattered through and around.

There was no danger of falling off the hull, Larry knew, but still he was just a bit nervous. Even if the magnetic shoes failed to hold, Newton's Laws of Motion assured him that he'd continue to drift along in the same direction and at the same speed as the ship. But, all the same, he'd rather do his space traveling *within* the ship, he decided.

That was what the small gun was for. It made him a miniature rocket of his own. A spaceship moves by propelling jets; the jets force fuel out, and the balancing reaction forces the ship forward. For every action, an equal and opposite reaction. The same law

18

that provides for the kickback of a revolver allows for the motion of a spaceship. And so with Larry's gun. In care he started to drift away from the ship, a bullet carefully fired would aim his drift back toward the ship.

It was O'Hare's whisper over the helmet-radio that brought him back and made him realize that he had been standing on the skin of the ship as if frozen, staring out into space. "Hsst, laddy. Work to do. Let's go!" O'Hare's deep voice was cold and metallic over the helmet-radio.

Slowly Larry worked his way across the ship's skin, following the tracks that led to the rear jets. O'Hare was up ahead, leading the way.

Larry walked gingerly along the steel tracks. The fact that he was Larry Stark, a twenty-year-old human being, had dropped away from him completely; he was Thor, he was Zeus, he was some Olympian god up here in the heavens, walking across his chariot. All around was his domain; here, in the blackness—

A bright flash and an amazed roar snapped him back to reality for the second time. In his helmet he heard an amazing string of curses.

"May the devil plague this thing! Going off in my hand! Help me, Larry! Help!"

O'Hare was drifting slowly away from the ship! Larry realized quickly what had happened. Somehow O'Hare's gun had gone off in his hand and had blasted him loose from the walking-tracks. The reaction, Newton's inevitable law, had set him going on a trajectory aimed away from the ship.

O'Hare was moving slowly, so slowly, drifting just overhead. Larry strained up, trying to reach the massive boot that hung above him, but it was just a few

19

inches from his grasp and drawing further away. A mixture of curses and prayers filled his ears.

Larry abandoned his attempt at grabbing O'Hare, for he knew that if should lose his own footing on the outside of the ship he would drift off in the same direction as the big Irishman.

"Use your gun, Pat!"

O'Hare stopped cursing for a moment. "That's just the trouble," he said. "I don't have it. And this old-fashioned suit doesn't have an extra like yours."

O'Hare's own gun was floating off into space in the opposite direction. The redhead had dropped it in his amazement when it fired, and it had kicked itself out into space. It was headed back toward Earth, while O'Hare gradually drifted out to the stars.

He was a hundred feet away when Larry thought of

the gun he held clutched in his space glove. O'Hare was moving slowly, swimming in space, unable to direct himself back to the ship which steadily moved farther and farther away.

His bull voice continued to crackle in Larry's receiver. "I guess it's fitting for an O'Hare to be dying out here in the stars," the giant was saying. "Better be it here than in bed like an old man, eh, laddy?"

"Just a minute, O'Hare," Larry called into his radio's transmitter. "I've got another gun here, you know."

"What? Saints be blessed, lad, can ye throw it straight? If ye can, fling it!"

"I'll try, Pat." Larry knew it would be tough. Not only did the throw have to be accurate—right at O'Hare —but he had to judge the velocity. If he threw too slowly, the gun would never catch up with O'Hare, and he would drift out forever toward the stars with his means of safety trailing just a few yards behind him. Or, if he threw too hard, it might swiftly fly past O'Hare before he could catch it.

It was the only thing Larry could do, though. He had been a pretty good pitcher, back in the days before he had traded his baseball uniform for his Space Cadet uniform.

He took careful aim, drew back his arm, and sent the gun flying out into space.

Tiny, dark, almost invisible, it drifted toward O'Hare. If only the aim were true enough, Larry hoped. The gun followed the inflexible path imparted to it by Larry's throw, passed an inch or two beyond O'Hare's desperate grasp, and continued on its way through space.

O'Hare watched it go, without ceasing his running chatter.

"If I don't get back, lad, tell Grennell to give you

my guitar, now that you know how to use it. And don't let that rascal be dragging you into any card games, either! And someday, Larry, when you're a captain and wear the Grays and can order people around like slaves, think of the tubemonkeys, and a big stupid redheaded Irishman who—"

"Quiet. There's one other thing I can do." And before he had a chance to reflect on what he was doing, he drew the extra gun from its clamp and fired it, throwing himself out into space in the general direction of O'Hare.

O'Hare gave a roar of surprise and anger, but Larry hardly noticed. Moving in space was something like swimming in ice, he found; space seemed frozen around him. But as he continued to move, he decided it was more like swimming in molasses. The ship lay behind him, an alarming distance away. The silver hull gleamed dully in the dark. Above and below him there was nothing but darkness sprinkled with bright hard stars.

Now he was approaching O'Hare. He saw he was going to miss the big man by almost ten degrees, and fired again to correct the error. The explosion of the gun made no sound, since there was no atmosphere to carry the sound waves, but the bright flash seemed to light up the galaxy.

The shot had the required effect. He floated straight at the waiting O'Hare, who extended one powerful arm and gathered him in.

"You fired two shots, didn't you?"

"Right."

"We have two left. They'd better be good ones. Give me the gun."

Larry very carefully handed the gun to O'Hare, who took it as if he were handling a soap bubble and secured it in his hand, completely hiding it in his great paw. Deftly he fired once, aiming them back, and slowly and surely they drifted back toward the *Carden*.

Moving in slow motion, they approached the ship and hovered some fifteen feet above it. There was not a sound in the universe; they might have been frozen in some cosmic photograph instead of moving and breathing and struggling. They stayed fifteen feet above the ship.

"No good," O'Hare said. "The ship's carrying us along now, and we won't get any closer. Here—hold on to me with your arms outstretched. Feet toward the ship. That's it."

O'Hare took both Larry's hands in one of his and extended him toward the ship feet-first. Then he fired the final shot.

They moved forward till Larry's feet hung in space just a few inches from the ship. Larry stretched until one shoe touched the walking strips and caught with a satisfying click. He reached up and hauled O'Hare down until he, too, was safely anchored to the skin of the ship.

They looked at each other. Through his helmet Larry saw that O'Hare's usually florid face had turned pale, and his breath was coming thick and heavy; Larry heard it in his radio.

Suddenly Larry felt very weak, very tired. He wanted to be back inside, safe and snug.

O'Hare clapped Larry on the back with a space-gloved hand. "Thanks, lad," he said. Even with the distortion of the helmet-radio Larry felt the gratitude flowing from the big tubemonkey.

They said nothing else, but gingerly edged along the ship to the jets in silence. The problem facing them seemed insignificant after the excitement just past, but Larry realized that the fate of the entire crew hung on O'Hare for the moment. If he couldn't perform the necessary repairs, perhaps no one could. And the *Carden* would drift on and on, slowly and steadily, while its crew starved within.

They reached the entrance to the tubes, and O'Hare paused.

"Wait here, Larry. I'll take care of it myself."

The big man disappeared around the curve and into the maw of the jets like a king striding to his throne room. Larry stood at the entrance and tried to peer into the darkness.

The stars all around were sharp points of hard light. There was no atmosphere, no dust to make them twinkle. Larry glanced up as if to stare at them as their conqueror; space had tried to get him, but he had overcome it.

After what must have been ten minutes, O'Hare's helmet loomed up over the lip of the tube, and the rest of him followed.

"I've fixed the trouble," O'Hare said. "Freakiest accident I've ever seen. We can go back inside now, Spaceman Stark."

CHAPTER 4

LARRY SHED his heroism as he entered the *Carden*. There were no heroes in the Patrol, only spacemen. Spacemen's ethics held that such a rescue was mere line-of-duty operation, not worth discussing. So Larry proceeded to forget the matter had even taken place, though he knew O'Hare would always remember.

The overdrive went back on without snag—O'Hare had done his job well—and the *Carden* resumed its journey toward Alpha Centauri at faster-than-light velocity.

Life aboard the *Carden* swung back to the familiar routine. Classes—by now, he thought, he could navigate a spaceship by himself—and chores, and exams,

25

and visits to the jet section, and long arguments with Harl.

O'Hare had taught Larry how to play the electronic guitar, and for hours during free time the two of them would sing together, would sing the plaintive ballads and roaring tunes developed during the two and a half centuries of space travel.

Occasionally O'Hare would sink into a sentimental mood and sing of Earth, its hills and lakes, its towering cities and its pretty girls. But those songs were few and far between: for the most part he sang of space, of the bold pioneers who left their corpses on the Moon in the twentieth century.

Now and then Larry would stop to think of the planet he had left behind. Not often, for it was hard to wrench himself from space. But he would look back at his home town, and at his friends and playmates, and wonder how he had been able to stand Earthbound life so long. For this, this was the real life, out here next to the stars!

They moved back out of overdrive on schedule the next day.

"We ought to hit the monitor station any minute," Harl said. "Shouldn't you be up front listening?"

"The captain said it wasn't necessary," Larry replied, looking up from his book. "We won't be in range of the monitor station for more than an hour"—he looked at his wristchron—"and I'll be back on duty by then."

The monitor station was an artificial satellite revolving around the sun Alpha Centauri. All spaceships bound for any of the planets of Alpha C checked in with the monitor station before landing.

Harl reached over and turned on his recorder. The sad, weary sounds of his favorite composition, Elsberry's "Dance by the Martian Sea," flowed into the room.

"That's your Martian thing, isn't it?" Larry asked.

"Yes," Harl said. "You don't mind my playing it?"

"Go right ahead. I was getting sick of studying anyway." He closed the book and dropped it.

"You don't like this piece much, eh, Larry?"

"I'm getting to. It's awfully old-fashioned, really, but I'm starting to like it."

"I'm glad. Martian music is a lot like Mars itself. No one likes it at first, but it grows on you till you can't help feeling it in every fiber of your body. That's why this piece means so much to me."

"Check," Larry said. "But maybe the music doesn't mean so much to people who aren't native Martians. Maybe—"

"Who said I'm a native Martian?" Harl interrupted. "I was born on Jupiter."

"Oh," Larry said. "*That* explains it." Larry had wondered why Harl was short and burly, while all the other Martians he had seen were tall and attenuated. Apparently he was part of the ill-fated colony which had struggled against the overpowering gravity of Jupiter for twenty-five years before admitting defeat.

"I was part of the Jupiter colony," Harl said. "I was born there and lived there for three or four years, enough time to develop these muscles. You mature early when you have to fight gravity nearly three times that of Earth."

"And you went to Mars when the colony broke up?"

"Right. My parents were killed in the Revolution. I lived with an older cousin who was a Martian colonist."

Larry was silent, fitting this new information into the pattern of what he already knew. He wondered

27

what Jupiter-born Harl Ellison was doing in the Patrol Academy. An Earth boy chosen for the Academy could not refuse the honor—who ever did?—but non-Terrans had the option of turning down the bid.

And Jupiter-born Harl Ellison, with his background, should have every reason to hate Earth and its colonial policies. The Jovians, Larry knew, had never understood why it had been necessary to evacuate the struggling colony on the huge planet. A Jovian would tell you that Earth had ruthlessly exploited the rich mineral mines on Jupiter, without offering any aid to the struggling colonists in return. Actually, Larry thought, we know that Earth poured so much money into Jupiter that it nearly wrecked its own economy and had to end the colonization. If the colonists had only understood this, it might have been possible to avoid the war in which the outraged colony finally revolted, refused to turn any minerals over to the Earth commissioner, and declared itself independent. They had been forcibly evacuated by a large Earth force, with many casualties as a result, and the Jupiter mines were now operated by convict labor.

"We've been away from home nearly a month," Harl said. "Another month or so more and we'll be officers in the Patrol at last."

"At last," Larry repeated. He thought of his father, stern and resplendent in his uniform, and of his old grandfather, still an upright and powerful man, and of the long line of Starks who had served Earth in the Space Patrol.

"I've waited a long time for this," Harl said. "I've always wanted to be a spaceman, and the Patrol is the ideal, for me. That and visiting Earth—I've never been there. But we'll have to go there to get our commissions, won't we?"

28

"That's right," Larry said. "As soon as we get back from Alpha C."

Harl nodded. "Alpha C. That's another of my ambitions coming true. You didn't think I was so ambitious, did you? I want to see the dinosaurs, and see the colony. I don't have to tell you how I feel about space colonies—I've been a colonist all my life."

"I heard some strange things about the Alpha C colony, though," Larry said. "Before I left some fellow was telling me about a book he'd read that said Alpha C ought to have its independence after all this time."

"You don't mean *No More Slavery*, do you?" Harl reached into his bag and hauled forth a blue paper-covered booklet. "This? Very fine book."

Larry looked at his bunkmate coldly. "Yes, that's the book. But I didn't expect to find a cadet reading it. You may come from a colony of rebels, but you knew what you were asking for when you joined the Patrol. Your loyalty belongs to Earth."

Harl put his finger across his lips and Larry realized he had been talking too loud. "Quiet. The neighbors'll think we're fighting. Hold on a minute, Larry. I'm as loyal to Earth as the next fellow. But I happen to think these fellows on Alpha C may be right when they say they ought to have their independence."

"If you think that you can't be loyal to Earth," Larry said. Inwardly he felt vaguely disturbed. In the month he had lived with Harl he had come to respect his judgment in many matters, to see that the powerful young Martian had a wide and intelligent view of things. And now here was Harl practically attacking Earth, which Larry had been taught to hold virtually sacred. Larry decided to cling to his loyalty; he had often bowed to Harl's keener judgment, but he would not now.

"If you'd only read the book, maybe you wouldn't think so. Earth can't always be right, Larry. Be objective about it. Here. Read the book and then we'll discuss the thing." He held out the book. Larry looked at it, almost reached for it.

"No. I don't want to read it. Earth's doing the right thing—the only thing—with Alpha C, and I don't want to bother reading something like this. Look, Harl. I understand how it is. Your parents had some friction with Earth when you were a baby, and you've always resented the Jupiter affair. But I'm sure it's you who's not being objective. Earth knows what it's doing on Alpha C, and I think it's right."

Harl was smiling oddly. Larry looked at his wrist-chron. "Hey! I'm due at the radio set in one minute." He snapped his shoesnaps and tidied his uniform. "Let's forget the whole thing, shall we, Harl? The whole argument never took place."

Harl nodded. "All right, Larry. If you want to. I'll put the book away. But if you ever want to read it, go right ahead. Maybe it'll open your eyes a little."

"Don't talk about opening my eyes. You're the one who's not seeing clearly." Larry left, but as he sped down the corridor toward the radio room strange doubts twisted in his mind. He wondered whether or not he ought to take a look at Harl's book after all. It couldn't do any harm, and his father wouldn't ever have to know. He turned off and headed for the radio set. Captain Reinhardt was waiting next to it as he entered.

CHAPTER 5

Just ON TIME, Cadet Stark," Reinhardt said in his staccato voice. "I've turned the machine on for you. We're within radio range of Alpha C now."

Larry sat down at the huge and complex machine which served for interplanetary communications. Ignoring the captain, who peered over his shoulder to make sure nothing went wrong, Larry turned dials, checked figures, and made hurried computations. Then, in the background, a soft but piercing noise started up from somewhere.

It swelled and swelled until it seemed to fill the room. Larry thought his brain would burst, but he gave no sign and sat at the machine making adjustments. Intercom was a science requiring great skill; Larry's aptitude test, taken when he was a recruit at

31

the Academy, showed that he promised to be a more than outstanding radio operator, and he had gone on to prove the test right.

Suddenly the noise ceased and was replaced by a dry, impersonal, metallic voice.

"Alpha Centauri Monitor Station X03216. Who is approaching, please?"

Larry gave the answering formula. "Spaceship *Carden,* out of Earth 15 June Earthtime, seeking entrance to London Colony on Alpha Centauri IV. Do we have clearance?"

The metallic voice was replaced by a more human one as the robot which had made the initial question gave way to the human operator who handled the station.

"Who's this? Mellillo?"

"No," Larry said. "Stark. New man."

"First trip, Stark? Name's Henry. Can't give you clearance, Stark. You'll have to get it from the local authorities on IV. I hear the London Colony spaceport is semiclosed."

Larry looked at Captain Reinhardt. "On whose authority?" the captain asked.

Larry said, "Captain Reinhardt of the *Carden* wants to know on whose authority they're closing up."

The Alpha Centauri operator replied, *"On their own, it seems. They've applied to the Interstellar Council for permission to close up, and in the meantime they've gone ahead and done it themselves. I think they're up to something down there."*

"Can we get clearance from them?"

"I suppose so, unless they just don't want company. I don't see how they can refuse a Patrol ship. Hold on while I try to make contact with the local operator."

32

A few minutes passed, and then a new voice came over the radio.

"*Operator Miller speaking from the Free World of Alpha Centauri IV. What is your request, please?*"

Larry turned in amazement and stared at the captain. "Free World of Alpha Centauri IV!"

"*What is your request, please?*" the operator repeated.

The captain signaled for Larry to get up. He did, and Captain Reinhardt slid smoothly into the seat.

"Captain Reinhardt of Earth ship *Carden* speaking. Request landing privileges at London Colony."

"*This is a semiclosed planet, Captain Reinhardt. Present regulations prohibit landing at London Colony.*"

Larry saw the captain begin to grow angry. "Semiclosed? Under whose authority?"

The reply was swift and even. "*Under the authority of the Council of the Free World of Alpha Centauri IV. Are you in need of repairs?*"

"No. This is a Space Patrol Training Cruise. May I be connected with the office of President Harrison, please?"

"*The President and his council are no longer located at London Colony.*"

Captain Reinhardt stared at the machine as if it were some live beast. He said nothing, only stared.

"Are you in revolt?" he snapped.

"*Landing on the Free World of Alpha C IV is prohibited temporarily,*" the operator repeated, ignoring the captain's question.

Suddenly a new voice cut in. "*You may land at Chicago Colony, Captain Reinhardt.*"

The London Colony operator made an attempt to scramble reception, but Larry quickly reached in front

33

of the captain and touched the dial that would prevent this.

"Who is speaking now?" asked Captain Reinhardt.

"Office of President Harrison, in Chicago Colony. You may land here, if you wish."

Captain Reinhardt frowned. Larry thought of Harl, of the little book Harl had, of the Jupiter colony.

"Yes. We'll land immediately."

"Very good, sir. President Harrison will be there to greet you when you land." He signed off.

Captain Reinhardt got up from the machine, signed to Larry to shut it off, and strode off to his cabin, his face creased with frowns, without saying a word.

Larry returned to his cabin. Harl was reading a book very intently, and listening to some early Earth music. He turned off the recorder as Larry entered.

"Well?"

"We're landing at Chicago Colony instead of London." Larry decided not to say any more. What he transmitted was supposed to be forgotten immediately by the operator, and he wasn't sure he wanted to repeat it to Harl anyway.

"I've computed an orbit while you were gone," Harl said. "We ought to hit Alpha C IV sometime tomorrow. We've already passed Alpha C I. And II and III are coming up."

"Certainly are a peculiar bunch of planets in this system. Alpha C I is normal enough—it's almost identical to Mercury. But II and III are funny ones."

"Are they the double ones? I'm pretty hazy about the planets in this system."

"Yes. The second and third planets revolve around each other. They're both about the size of Mars, and completely unsuitable for human life."

34

"How come?"

"The two planets are so close to each other that the tides are completely mad, and there are regular floods that cover the whole planet in sections. If there ever is a colony there they'd have to be nomads, wandering around just ahead of the floods."

"And it could never be self-sufficient," Harl said. "They wouldn't be able to raise any crops."

That part always interested Harl, Larry thought. He wanted every colony to be self-sufficient. Larry was becoming more and more perplexed by his friend; he wanted to believe that Harl was loyal to Earth and the Patrol, but he was beginning to feel he was not.

"What's the rest of the system like, Larry?"

"Well, IV is the planet most suited for human life, because of the atmosphere. It's almost like Earth's." Larry reached for one of their textbooks and flipped through it. "Let's see. Then there's V, which is the same size as Earth but which has an atmosphere of poisonous gases, and VI, which is pretty cold but which has a tiny colony planted there."

"Colony?" Harl looked extremely interested. "I didn't know about that. What does the book say about them?"

"Hmm. It's pretty tiny. At last report it's about twelve people living in a pressure dome."

"It's a start," Harl said, laughingly.

"Alpha C VII and VIII are giant planets," Larry continued. "Too heavy to support human life or even to allow any humans to land there. Sort of a super-Jupiter, you might say."

"I remember reading about those two," Harl said. "Two exploratory ships landed on VII about twenty years ago, but the pull of gravity was so strong they couldn't lift the ship up once it landed. In fact they

35

couldn't do anything at all—the gravity plastered them to the ground, and they just stuck there till they starved to death. Typical Patrol foul-up."

"You'd almost think you didn't want to be in the Patrol," Larry said, looking down at Harl. "The way you keep talking as if—"

"Never mind," Harl said. "I thought you had a sense of humor, but you're awfully touchy when it comes to the Patrol."

Larry flushed. He saw that once again Harl was right. He was acting pretty stuffy about the Patrol. "Sorry, Harl. I don't mean to keep harping like that."

"Forget it. What does your book say about native life on these planets?"

"Nothing much. We can't tell if there's any life on VII and VIII, of course, but the gravity is so strong that probably nothing can stand up to it but some sort of jellyfish. And planets IX, X, and XI are too cold to support any form of life at all. There's aquatic life on II and III, and primitive snow animals on VI. It's too hot on I, and we haven't found anything on V so far. You know about IV."

"I sure do," Harl said. "Who doesn't?"

Larry closed the book and tried to picture Alpha C IV in his mind. They would land tomorrow; tonight he could see it in imagination only. Alpha C IV was a lush, young, tropical world. Here and there the jungles were dotted with Earth colonies. But the planet was green and primitive, and its natives were giant dinosaurs. Larry wondered if you could hear the ground shake when they came near.

CHAPTER 6

AT MIDDAY on July 16 the *Carden* hung just outside the atmospheric blanket of the fourth planet of the sun Alpha Centauri. Guided by a base on the planet, the ship entered a landing orbit and spiraled down.

Twenty miles from planetfall, a small ship from Chicago Colony came out to meet them and guide them down through the atmosphere. The two ships landed on a field just outside Chicago Colony. A small group of colonists was waiting for them as they came out of the ship.

The first thing that struck Larry was the strong pull of gravity. Alpha C IV was a big world, he recalled; its diameter was nearly ten thousand miles, as compared with Earth's own seven thousand miles. Thus,

Larry reasoned, the natives—no, he corrected himself, not the natives but the colonists—would all be heavy and muscular, their muscles developed from fighting the strong gravity. A look at the Centaurans confirmed this.

The next thing that struck him was the atmosphere. He sucked in a chestful of air and reluctantly exhaled it; Harl, he saw, was doing the same thing, as were all the spacemen. Not since leaving Earth had they breathed real air. On Mars he and his shipmates had breathed the artificial air of the dome, not the thin, sharp, low-oxygen Martian air outside. On Pluto there was no air outside the dome; it all lay frozen on the rocks. And the *Carden,* like the Mars and Pluto domes, used artificially restored air. Larry had almost forgotten what real air tasted like.

Alpha C IV had no domes. Everything was out under the sky, in the real air. Larry pulled in a sharp breath.

After a month, breathing natural air was luxury. The air on Alpha C IV was sweet, almost dizzying—it's the oxygen, Larry thought. Slightly greater oxygen content than Earth air—but above all else, it was fresh. Stepping from the ship into this air was almost a physical shock, as the clean new air poured into his lungs.

They walked quickly from the ship to where an immense wall loomed up before them—at least a hundred feet it rose into the air, perhaps more. All around he saw lush vegetation, strange green plants that towered high overhead.

"Those walls keep out the native animals," explained a muscular-looking colonist who was leading them. "Each of the four settlements is surrounded by a similar wall, and so far none of the big beasts has gotten through."

38

Larry looked around. He knew he was on a young world, still in the stage known as Mesozoic on Earth. The dominant form of life was the giant reptile, just as it had been on Earth hundreds of millions of years before.

Down at the bottom of the huge wall was a tiny gate, a bare six feet high, through which none of the great beasts could possibly enter. The little party of Earthmen followed through the gate and into the Chicago Colony.

It was a busy place. Larry saw stores, markets, homes. It looked as any other frontier town might look. There was none of the gleaming chrome which decorated Earth's cities, none of the sharp functional lines. Chicago Colony seemed a simple, almost primitive place.

They followed the guide through the streets. Captain Reinhardt walked next to him and was talking in a low whisper. A few colonists gathered in clumps and stared with open curiosity.

"Look at the streets," Larry whispered to Heitor van Haaren, a short, chubby cadet who had bunked on the other side of the corridor. "I think they're paved with concrete."

"Maybe they can't afford plastine," Heitor suggested.

"Maybe they don't want it," Harl said. "It's not as durable as concrete."

"That's true," Heitor said. "Plastine has to be replaced every few years."

The guide turned off into an imposing building and the Earth party followed him. They climbed a flight of stairs—a strange experience for Earthmen accustomed to escalators and power lifts—and entered a large room.

A white-haired, distinguished-looking man was waiting there for them, simply dressed in an old-fashioned style. He rose and walked toward them as they entered.

"I'm Harrison," he said. "President of the Colonial Council. In exile," he added in a lower voice.

Captain Reinhardt introduced himself and some of his party quickly, and seemed to be about to say something else when President Harrison interrupted.

"Are you people hungry?" Harrison asked abruptly.

Larry felt like saying "yes" himself, he was so hungry. But Captain Reinhardt surprised him by replying, "Why, yes, we are." It would have been more like him to take care of official business first.

"Then let's eat first and talk later," Harrison said.

He led the way to a dining room and indicated that they were to take seats around the table. He sat down between Larry and Captain Reinhardt.

They ate in silence. A few colonists joined them at the table: all, like Harrison, were heavy-set, silent men. None of the food was familiar to Larry, who was accustomed to concentrates and synthetics.

The main course was some sort of steak, tough but flavorous. Larry had just finished his piece when President Harrison turned to him and said, without prologue, "Did you like the meat?"

"Very much, sir," said Larry, somewhat suprised. It was the first thing Harrison had said since the meal began.

"Good to hear it. Some of our visitors aren't too fond of our dinosaur steaks."

"Dinosaur steaks!" Larry stared at his plate in amazement, and several of the spacemen smothered laughter.

"It's our major food here," Harrison went on. "We only have about a thousand people in Chicago Colony,

40

so two or three dinosaurs can feed most of us for a week. Those statues you saw outside were carved from 'saur bones."

Then Harrison turned back to his plate and finished in silence. When the meal was over he signaled to the Earthmen to follow him back to the large room.

Suddenly he said, "I'm glad you came, Captain Reinhardt. We've had a lot of trouble here, and we're going to have more. But I didn't want to call the Patrol because I want to settle this thing peacefully."

"What are you talking about, President Harrison? I've heard some strange things. Why did you move from London Colony to Chicago Colony, for example? What's going on here?" The captain was frowning. It seemed to Larry that he would rather discuss these things in private with Harrison, and was annoyed at having to talk in front of all his men and the other colonists.

President Harrison sat back in his chair. "You know, of course, that there is a motion on the floor of the Interstellar Council that will give independence to the Alpha C IV colony within twenty-five years, provided the colonists can show unified self-government."

"I'm aware of that," said Captain Reinhardt. Larry and Harl exchanged glances. The men from Earth watched quietly, listening to every word.

"Why should that make the people of Alpha C IV— ah—unfriendly to the people of Earth?" the captain asked.

"A group of hotheads in London Colony decided that this bill would be an excuse for putting off our independence indefinitely, on the grounds that we would never be considered ready for self-government. They took over the rule of London Colony and forced me to come here."

41

"What about Henrikstown? And Bombay Colony? Have they gone over also?"

"Probably. Chicago Colony is the only one of the four still loyal to Earth."

Captain Reinhardt stood up and paced angrily up and down. "This is preposterous. Where's the Resident Governor? Why hasn't he done something about it?"

"The London Colony people have sent him back to Earth, Captain." President Harrison's voice dropped. "By regular drive. They gave him a five-year food supply."

The *Carden* men were shocked, but even so a few of them chuckled, Harl the loudest. Larry had to admit it was a clever stroke, packing the Earth Resident Governor off to his home planet in a ship that wouldn't arrive for years. But it was an even more serious matter than exiling the local government.

"And you didn't notify me? You should have informed Earth immediately."

Harrison smiled like a small boy caught doing something wrong. "I intended to, Captain Reinhardt. But then I was told the *Carden* was approaching, and I waited for you before I did anything."

The captain continued to pace up and down. Larry felt anger beginning to grow within him. These colonists—even the loyal ones like Harrison—had managed to make fools of Earth and had spurned Earth's offer to let them have their independence. But Larry felt sure they would soon be put back in their place by the Patrol.

"What's the sentiment in Chicago Colony about joining the other three?"

"About half and half. They're holding a meeting tomorrow night to decide which they want to do, support Earth or the revolutionaries."

"We'll stop that quick enough. Get me the leader of the local revolutionaries. Olcott," he said, turning to his pilot, "announce that Chicago Colony is now under martial law. The rest of you get to whatever quarters these colonists have provided. I want to talk to Harrison some more."

The men from the *Carden* were conducted to a building near the edge of town, and Harl, Larry, and Heitor van Haaren were given a large, bare room to themselves. There was one window, and it looked outward over the great wall, so one could see the jungle beyond.

"Do you think there's going to be any fighting?" Heitor asked as soon as they got settled. Larry smiled. He had known Heitor slightly at the Academy; he was a rotund, slow-moving boy, a brilliant student who had often baffled his professors with scientific points beyond their comprehension. Larry knew that Heitor would prefer as little fighting as possible.

"I don't know," Larry admitted. "They'll probably call in the nearest Patrol destroyer if there's any trouble, and pack us right back to Earth."

"It looks like a pretty good fight shaping up," Harl said. "It reminds me of what I was told about the early days of the Jupiter revolution. They followed the same pattern, and it turned into a full-scale war."

"I hope they can prevent it here," Larry said. "These Centaurans look like good hard-working people. It would be too bad if we had to fight them."

"Yes," Harl said, laughing softly as he walked to the window. "It's too bad these good hard-working people don't have sense enough to let Earth sit on their necks forever, eh, Larry? Just like the Martians, and the Jupiter people before them."

43

"Hold on!" Larry said. "What do you mean, Earth sitting on their necks? I don't like the way you've been talking, Harl. Earth's been helping this colony along since it started, and they just want to get their investment back. If it weren't for Earth none of the colonies could get started."

"That's right. But if it weren't for Earth all the colonies would be rich independent planets now, instead of piddling little mudholes! I don't know, Stark. I guess that's what comes of coming from a long line of Space Patrol people. Your family's filled your head full of so much nonsense about Earth that you don't know—"

"You can't talk like that," Larry snapped, and moved menacingly toward Harl. The burly Martian waited for him, but Heitor interposed.

"Hold on, you two. If you want to have your own private war, go outside and do it. Or work off your feelings hunting dinosaurs. I'm tired, and I want to sleep."

"Heitor's right, Larry. We're acting pretty silly."

"I suppose we are." He held out his hand and Harl grasped it. "You could be a great guy," Larry said. "If only you didn't—"

"That'll be enough," Harl said, giving Larry a gentle tap on the arm with his fist. "We'll talk about it some other time. Suppose we get some sleep."

CHAPTER 7

ON HIS first morning on Alpha C IV Larry awoke early. The cadets had left the window wide open, and the warm, sweet air drifted in and hung in the room like perfume.

He got up silently—Harl and Heitor were still asleep —and walked to the window. He stared out over the wall. There was a clearing in which the *Carden* was standing, just as it had been left. And stretching around behind the clearing was a tangled forest of great weird green trees, hundreds of feet high.

The trees were not the familiar maples and oaks of home, though Larry saw an occasional tree looking something like an ordinary pine standing in the midst of the strangeness.

Suddenly he noticed a commotion in the trees. The

closely packed branches began to wave back and forth and thresh around. Larry stretched on tiptoes to get a better view of whatever was going on. The early morning sun was over the wall by now, and all was as quiet as it always is just an hour after dawn.

The disturbance in the trees grew more frantic, and then abruptly the trees parted and something ambled out into the clearing. Larry gasped. It was the biggest animal he had ever seen.

Keeping one eye on the window as if he feared the animal would disappear if he looked away, Larry backed to Harl's bed and grabbed the bare foot that stuck out from under the covers. He shook it a couple of times.

"Go away," Harl murmured sleepily. "Go away."

"Wake up!" Larry whispered. "Look out the window!"

"What do you want?" mumbled Harl. He slowly pushed the covers off and almost fell out of bed. Larry led him, still half asleep, to the window. They looked out.

Harl was silent for a minute. Then he rubbed his eyes and said, "Pinch me. I'm still asleep."

"No you're not," laughed Larry. "That's one of the natives of this planet, that's all. How'd you like to have him for a pet?"

They stared. The huge reptile in the clearing was dull gray in color, and long. It had four ponderous legs and a hugh neck, at the end of which was a tiny head. Tiny by comparison with the rest of the body, that is. Behind the massive body a tail studded with spines swept away into the jungle.

There was no way of telling the size of the beast, but it was immense.

"It's going near the ship!" Harl said. The monster

46

was cautiously approaching the *Carden,* which stood upright and gleaming in the morning light. Each step the animal took seemed to be a drumbeat far off. The ground shook under him.

Heitor, awakened by the conversation, left his bed and came to the window. There wasn't room for all three of them, and they jostled for position to see what was happening.

The dinosaur had come close to the empty ship now. It lifted its huge neck and gently nuzzled the cold side of the ship—probably, Larry thought, wondering what sort of animal it was dealing with. Then it continued its explorations until it reached the door at the top of the catwalk—the door sixty-five feet above the ground.

With great care it pushed the door open with the tip of its nose, and put a giant eye to the open door. Apparently it saw nothing, for it lowered its head again, slowly marched once around the *Carden,* and, puzzled, turned tail and ponderously strode off once again into the jungle.

The Earthmen assembled downstairs in a long room ringed with the stuffed heads of bizarre native animals. Several of the other men had seen the dinosaur approach the ship also, and the incident was a topic of general discussion until Captain Reinhardt entered the room. He was followed by President Harrison and two Centauran soldiers, escorting a slender, dark-skinned young colonist.

"This is Jon Browne," President Harrison said. "He's the leader of the local revolutionary faction."

Captain Reinhardt looked at the young man coldly. "Stand over there, Browne. I want to question you."

Larry surveyed the scene. He wished he could understand what motivated Browne, why he wanted to

47

break loose from Earth. Whatever reasons he might have, Larry thought, they could never be sufficient.

But he didn't like Captain Reinhardt's overbearing attitude much either, he reflected. He had admired the stern military man at first, but as the voyage had gone along he had almost begun to dislike him.

Browne walked cockily over to the place the captain indicated and stood there awaiting questioning.

"I understand you're holding a town meeting here tonight," the captain said. "For what reason?"

"Are you going to hold any of this against me, Captain? I don't want to testify against myself, you know."

"Don't worry about that. Why this meeting tonight?"

"Very well," Browne said. "You know about the other three colonies, don't you? Tonight I'm going to ask that Chicago Colony join the other three. And if I don't do it, someone else will. Only a united planet can win independence for us from the people of Earth, who neither care about us nor about our liberty, but just about our taxes—"

"That'll be enough, Browne," the captain broke in. "You know, of course, that Chicago Colony is now under martial law and that I can prevent this meeting from ever being held?"

"That's violating free speech," Larry whispered in amazement to Harl.

"Shhh," Harl said. "Listen to them."

"Very true, Captain. But that would not prevent Chicago Colony from revolting."

"Suppose you tell me why Alpha C IV suddenly wants to be free, Browne."

The young colonist's eyes flashed. "Not suddenly, Captain Reinhardt. We've wanted to be free as long as we've been here. But now our dependence on Earth

48

is over; we're self-sufficient. Can't you understand that we don't need Earth, and Earth doesn't need us? They just cling to us for our taxes and in case they might need us some day. Earth gets no benefit from this colony, really—the taxes we send mean nothing to her economy. No; it's just greed and fear that makes you cling to us!"

"That's not true," Captain Reinhardt snapped. "Commerce is—"

"Commerce? Across four light-years? We're too far away for any particular commerce. It's all we can do to get the books and tools Earth can supply us."

"But if you rebel," said President Harrison, "you'll cut off your last supplies of these things."

"We can manage. We are a free people," said Browne, "and we should be free to carry on our own experiments in self-government, without the necessity of reporting our every action to Earth, without the necessity of paying taxes to Earth for the privilege of being governed by them."

"That's a quote from the book I have," Harl whispered to Larry. "Most of this stuff comes straight out of it."

Larry said nothing. He was deep in thought, trying to find some way out of his confusion. All his life he had been taught that Earth was noble, Earth was good, the protector of the colonies, the aider of the weak. For the first time that faith was being questioned, and he was very worried.

Captain Reinhardt sat silently, his jaws clamped. A few other colonists had filtered into the room and were standing near the door, and he looked at them uneasily. Browne went on arguing, as if the captain could give the Alpha C her independence by himself.

"Earth's trade restrictions hamper us. Their taxes

49

are a burden we shouldn't have to pay. We have no representation on the Interstellar Council anyway, and —maybe you know your Earth history, Captain Reinhardt. Six hundred years ago a colony of another nation on Earth was in the same position. What did they say? No Taxation without Representation? Remember those words, Captain?"

"I have heard them," Captain Reinhardt said stiffly.

"Don't they mean anything to you? This colony is ready to stand on its own feet as an independent planet," Browne shouted, "and you can tell that to your Council when you get back. Sure, they plan to give us independence—when they're good and ready!"

"How does he know they won't?" Larry asked.

"He knows his history better than you do," Harl said. "The Council never gives anything up till they don't have any choice."

"If you'd only be patient," President Harrison said.

"You tell us to be patient!" Browne shouted. "You tried to tell that to London Colony, and they threw you out. Now you're here and trying to tell us we should wait and not act by ourselves. Why? Do you want to save your own miserable job, Harrison? You're wrong and London Colony's right! We have to proclaim our independence—all four colonies."

Captain Reinhardt stood up. "I think that's enough," he said. "I see the picture more clearly now. I would like to settle this peacefully, if I could—you could tell your people that, Harrison. I will try to negotiate before I call in the armed might of the Patrol to put down the revolution. In the meantime, I think we'll keep this man"—he indicated Browne—"in our custody."

Several of the colonists standing at the door began to

edge forward menacingly. President Harrison turned to the captain.

"No," he said. "Arresting Browne would be the worst thing we could do. If we let him go, all he can do is talk. If we arrest him we'll be making a martyr out of him. It might be a very dangerous situation."

Captain Reinhardt scowled. "You're right. I hate to let him go, but there's nothing else we can do. What do you think is wisest about tonight's meeting?"

"Let it go on as scheduled," Harrison said. "It'll only make official what we know already. Canceling it might touch off something serious."

The captain nodded. "All right, take him out and let him go. Harrison, come with me. I want the background of this whole affair, from the beginning."

They left. The others, who had witnessed the discussion with some amazement, straggled slowly out of the hall, conscious that something big was brewing and also aware that as long as the captain remained in conference they were free.

Harl began to walk out quickly. Larry caught his sleeve.

"Wait a minute, Harl. Let's go upstairs—I want to look at that book of yours."

Harl's face reflected surprise. But he shook his head. "Some other time, Larry. I want to find that fellow Browne. I want to talk to him."

And he dashed out, leaving Larry standing by himself.

CHAPTER 8

HEITOR CAME up behind Larry as he stood there, and nudged him out of his reverie.

"Hey, Larry. What say we take advantage of our free time to explore the town?"

"Good enough," Larry said. He and Heitor headed out into the street.

They were in a business district, apparently; the street in front of them was a long line of shops.

"What did you think of Browne?" Heitor asked as they crossed to one of the shops.

"I don't know, Heitor. What he says seems to make sense, but I'm sure if we looked at Earth's side of the matter too—"

"Yes. I wish I knew why Earth has to treat its colonies like that," Heitor said.

52

They entered the first store. It seemed to specialize in carvings from dinosaur bones. The proprietor, an elderly but still powerful-looking man, came out to meet them.

"Welcome! I'm honored to have Earth visitors!" His accent was strange; the vowels were blurred, in a way, so it was somewhat difficult to understand him. What he seemed to be saying was, "Wilcam! Ay'm hanared ta hove Eerth vesetars!" This dialect, Larry knew, was the result of decades of isolation, during which time the pronunciation of the colonists had wandered further and further away from that of Earth.

Larry picked up an exquisite carving of some native animal. "Is this all you sell?" he asked.

"Yes, sir. Bone carving is our most important local art, and most of the artists in Chicago Colony use my shop as their outlet."

"Look at this one," Heitor said, holding up a four-inch representation of an odd-looking beast with a curling tail. "Real cute."

"You wouldn't think so if you saw him in the flesh," the old man said. "He's about eighty feet high and thirty feet long, and he eats young chaps like you for afternoon snacks."

"What's his name?"

"Wouldn't help if I told you. The names vary from settlement to settlement, and you Earthmen have your own names for them as well. I can't even pronounce your name for it," he said.

"How much do you want for this one?" said Heitor.

"Normally, about three solars. But you probably don't have any local currency anyway, and I prefer to trade."

"Trade?"

"Yes," the storekeeper said. "Suppose we swap

even-up—the statue for that book under your arm. We have so few books here."

"I'm afraid I can't do that," Heitor said. "This is one of my textbooks." He opened the book and showed its contents. "I need it to study from—it's very important."

Larry smiled. He had come to like Heitor much more in the past few days than ever before, probably because his frequent arguments with Harl had taken some of the ease out of his friendship with him. And this was so much like Heitor, who clung to his textbooks at all times and would rather part with a finger than an astrogation text.

The old man sighed. "Well, in that case I guess we can't swap. Look here—suppose you just take this as a gift from me. From Chicago Colony."

"Why—thank you." Heitor picked up the little statuette and stroked the polished ivory.

Larry looked admiringly at the object, wondering how he could find one as pretty. It would look good on his desk at home, he thought.

Home. It was the first time in days that he had even let the word enter his mind. Home was Earth, far across the sea of space. The distance was so vast it was meaningless. Twenty-five million million miles away.

They turned to leave, staring at the eight-foot statue of a dragonlike animal that stood near the entrance. Larry opened the door, then turned around.

"Say, old man. Is that meeting tonight open to Earthmen too? I think I'd like to come."

The storekeeper smiled slowly. "It won't concern you at all, lads. Better forget about it."

Another store was selling some strange-looking vegetables. The shopkeeper there gave Larry a small, round, red fruit which looked something like an Earth apple. He tasted it. It was bitter, tangy, strange.

Walking on Alpha C IV was almost difficult. Each step was a small battle; after ten or twelve steps, the cadets began to breathe a little harder. The air was rich and mysterious.

There was no sign in the settlement of the wild jungle which was rampant just outside the walls. The heavy vegetation was under control, and just a few weird trees with scaly bark served as reminders of the wild forest which lay without the walls.

Larry thought it was almost possible to feel as if he were back on Earth when he forgot about the gravity. But one glance into the clear blue sky dispelled any such thoughts.

The sun Alpha Centauri hung high and beat hot and yellow overhead. It seemed just a bit larger and hotter than the sun of Earth. But—in one corner of the sky hung pale Beta Centauri, the companion sun, a small circle of light. And over at the other side, down near the horizon, was the tiny red ball of Proxima Centauri, the other nearby star.

The sunlight was yellow, as on Earth. But mingling with it was the ghostly beam from Beta C and the trickle of crimson from Proxima. The overall effect was one of almost overpowering strangeness.

The cadets sat down on a bench, thankfully, since they were tired from fighting the heavier gravity of Alpha C IV. After a moment or two, Larry looked up to see Jon Browne standing nearby.

His face turned red and hot. He knew he was in the presence of a sworn enemy of the planet he held most dear—but he was unable to dislike him as he knew he should. Browne was a quite unferocious-looking, pleasant-faced young fellow.

"I don't think we were introduced," Browne said, opening the conversation in the abrupt way characteristic of the colonists. "But I think you saw me this morning. My name is Browne—with an 'e' at the end." He smiled. "Jon Browne."

"We saw you this morning," Larry said.

"Yes," Heitor agreed.

"Are you coming to the meeting tonight? It's open to you Earthmen, you know. But maybe you don't want to. I fear you've heard all there is to hear already, when I spoke with your captain."

"We'd like to come," Larry said. "At least, I would."

"So would I," Heitor said. "You know, I recall a song about someone with the same name as you. It's an old Earth song."

Larry nodded in recollection. It was a song O'Hare had taught him one night.

"It's some sort of political song," Heitor said. "It begins, 'John Brown's body lies a-moulderin' in the grave—'"

"An ancestor of mine, maybe?" said Jon Browne. "Maybe."

It developed that Browne was a second-generation colonist; his father had come from Earth about 2320, and he himself had been born on Alpha C IV.

"I have some free time now," he said. "Would you two like to climb the wall with me? It means some exercise, but if we're lucky you'll get a good view of our jungle. I understand you saw one of our 'saurs this morning nosing around your ship. What did you think of it?"

Larry drew in his breath. Finally he said, simply, "It's big."

Browne laughed. "You saw one of the biggest of all this morning. The scientists call it by a name half as long as the animal itself, but the colonists here call it twotails because the neck is so long it seems like a tail." He waved his arms to illustrate.

"Well, anyone joining me for a climb?"

"I'm game," said Larry. "How about you, Heitor?"

Heitor shook his head. "I'm beat. You two go climb your wall; I'm going to rest awhile and then head back to quarters to see what's going on. Anyway, I have some studying to do."

"O.K.," Larry said. He and Browne got up and walked off toward the wall.

Browne was likable enough, Larry decided. He made up his mind he would ignore the fact that he was going for a walk with the revolutionary leader. Jon Browne would be just another colonist to him.

"How much do you know about our planet, Larry?"

"What? Oh—well, that there are four settlements, called London Colony, Bombay Colony, Henrikstown, and Chicago Colony. That there are about five thousand humans on the whole planet, with about half of them in London Colony."

"Not quite half, Larry. Two thousand is more like it, and a thousand in each of the others."

They walked on for a while, till they approached the wall.

"How old is the colony?" Larry asked.

"Oh, about a hundred years—no, make it a hundred twenty-five. The first batch of settlers had trouble adjusting to the heavy grav, but it doesn't bother us any more. Our chief food comes from those big beasts out there—that's our chief problem, too. Until we get the 'saurs under control we can't have a true planet-wide culture. But when we do we'll have to substitute other sources of food. But we'll manage; don't worry."

At the base of the wall was a staircase cut into the stone and winding up to the top. They began to climb, Browne first, Larry behind.

"Do the 'saurs wander around the clearing very much?" Larry asked, panting a little as he climbed the stairs.

"Usually just early in the morning," said Browne. "Those twotails are so timid that the city noises usually scare them away after dawn. You were lucky to see one."

"Timid, you say?"

"That's right. They just eat grass, and they have to spend almost all day eating because they have such small heads. In order for them to pack away enough food to fill that big body, they have to spend ten or twelve hours a day just eating."

"Are all your 'saurs too scared to bother you?" Larry asked.

Browne chuckled. "Hardly, friend. Some of them would hop over the wall and eat us alive if they could. Maybe we'll see some of the dangerous kind while you're here."

They reached the top of the wall. Larry looked down at the ground two hundred feet away, with a few tiny people walking back and forth on the distant streets below. Then he walked across the top of the wall and peered cautiously over the other side.

The view was breathtaking. He saw a great green forest spreading away on all sides, wild, untamed, with strange leathery birds flapping above it. Directly below was the clearing in which the *Carden* stood, and not far away was the edge of the jungle. The nearest trees were almost as high as the wall.

"What's that?" Larry asked, pointing to one of the great birds which was hovering over a treetop.

"It's a wingfinger," said Browne. "Sort of a flying reptile, with those wings stretched out on its fingers, which are eight or nine feet long. The scientists call them pterodactyls, and they're just like a kind which once lived on Earth."

"Do they ever fly over the city?"

"They used to," said Browne. "For a while it was a serious problem—the wingfingers used to swoop low over the city, and there's a legend that one of them once carried off a child—but we shoot them on sight, and they've learned their lesson by now. They're afraid of us. They never come near the city."

The wingfinger was hovering over a treetop. Suddenly it's long beak pounced on a branch and emerged with a wriggling snake held tight. Triumphantly it flew off to enjoy its meal.

Larry shuddered. Browne said, "That's the way it is in the jungle. The wingfingers are always lying in wait for the tree snakes, and they manage to catch enough to keep well fed. But now and then a wingfinger will swoop too low over a lake and get dragged down by a water reptile with long arms."

A large dinosaur with ferocious teeth appeared at the edge of the clearing. Larry turned to point it out to Browne, but the colonist was peering at his wrist-chron.

"Getting late," he said. "I have to get back and prepare for the meeting. Do you want to stay here by yourself?"

The shadows of early afternoon were beginning to fall. Larry pictured himself on top of the wall at dusk, with the wingfingers humming by overhead. "No, thanks. I'll go back down with you."

"Fine," he said. "Will I see you at the meeting?"

"Most likely," Larry said. He followed Browne down the steps silently. Apparently these revolutionaries were pretty human people, Larry thought. He would have to get a look at that book of Harl's when he got back.

CHAPTER 9

THE PLACE was in turmoil when he returned. There were colonists all over the building, some demanding to speak to Captain Reinhardt, some just trying to make their feelings heard to anyone who would listen. Larry reported in to the captain, who was sitting at the dinner table talking in a low voice to Harrison and two other colonists, but Reinhardt signaled to him that he did not want to be disturbed.

Feeling that he was being left out of everything, Larry headed upstairs to his room. Heitor was in one corner, studying, and Harl was sprawled in the other, also reading. They looked up as he entered.

"Hi," said Harl. "O'Hare was in here looking for you before, but Heitor said you were out walking with Jon Browne. Did I hear straight?"

"That you did," Larry said. "We're invited to the town meeting tonight."

"Are you going?" Heitor asked.

"Unless Reinhardt needs us. But so far this trip it seems he needs us like a Martian sandstorm," Larry said. "Except when there's a floor to be scrubbed."

"Or a message to send," Harl said. "But you're not serious about going, are you?"

"Sure," Larry said. "Why not? I'm curious to see what happens. We've got history being made right in front of us, you know."

"True enough," Harl said. "But if they vote to rebel the first thing they may do is lynch the nearest Earthmen, if Browne stirs them up enough."

Larry looked at Harl in amazement. "You're kidding! I spent the afternoon with Browne, and he seems a perfectly fine fellow. I don't think he'd do any such thing."

"Treason!" Harl exclaimed, in mock oratorical style. "I accuse you of treason, Cadet Stark! What do you mean by complimenting a rebel? Someone who is risking his life to overthrow the colonial rule of Earth? Isn't he a vile creature, completely evil? That's what you seemed to be saying up to now, and naturally I believed you."

"Naturally," Larry said, with a smile. Harl's sarcasm was not lost on him. He sank into the nearest chair, considerably puzzled. What Harl was saying was right —he had thought of the revolutionaries as little more than criminals until meeting Browne and the other townspeople. Now he wasn't sure what to think at all. Enemies were beginning to look like friends, friends like enemies. He remembered what his father had often told him: "Always remember, Larry. Earth knows what it's doing. Don't let anyone fool you."

But were they fooling him? Was Earth all-wise and the colonists doing something wild and rash, or were they merely honest people fighting for their rights and Earth the blind oppressor? He wondered.

There was a knock on the door. Larry, glad of the interruption, leaped up to see who was there.

It was O'Hare. Larry looked up at the face of the big man, who had been his first friend among the spacemen. Under his arm O'Hare was carrying the treasured electronic guitar which he had taught Larry to play. O'Hare handed the guitar to Larry, who took it gently and cradled it in his arms.

"I think it's about time I give this to you, Larry," O'Hare said. Larry noticed that his face seemed pale, making his flaming red hair all the brighter by contrast. His eyes were deeper, even more intense than usual, and he had a strange grim look on his face.

"Why, Pat? I—" Larry looked at the instrument, then at O'Hare. It was an expensive, carefully built guitar with remarkable sound, and Larry knew it had been O'Hare's companion on many a voyage.

"It's just that I think you ought to have it, that's all," O'Hare said, speaking somewhat quickly. "I have to go now, laddy. A friend of mine's waiting for me. But I'll be back soon enough to hear you play it. You've got the makings of a good man with a guitar, Larry. I've often thought it a pity that you'll be a Patrolman instead of a tubemonkey. Such talents are wasted on the Patrol. But keep the guitar well, Larry. It's served me well for many years now, and I'd hate to see it kept poorly. You know how to tune it."

"Yes, O'Hare."

"And if you have any trouble with it, well—bring it along and come to see me. So long, Larry."

He opened the door, and walked out quickly.

63

"So long, Pat. And thanks," Larry said to the closing door.

"Strange," Larry said. "Why'd he do that?"

"Maybe he doesn't have room for it," Heitor suggested.

Larry shook his head. "He'd sooner make room for his guitar than for one of his legs. No, there must be some other reason."

"He'll tell you soon enough, if he wants to," Harl said. "Let's hear this fabulous instrument, anyway. I've heard some fine guitar-playing in my day—think you can match it?"

"I'll try," Larry said. He made the connection, and, as the guitar warmed up, he tried some preliminary strums.

A weird distorted noise came forth. Harl and Heitor dissolved in laughter.

"Very good, Professor Stark!" Harl said. "Now play us your next selection!"

Larry looked down at the guitar. He had never heard it so badly out of tune.

He strummed it again, and the sound was even worse.

"I think he dumped a sour job on you," Harl said. "Or maybe he's playing games."

"He's not the game-playing kind," Larry said. He fingered the fine controls on the guitar, trying to restore the sound. There was no improvement.

"It seems to be in tune. But the sounds are coming out sour."

"I know," Larry said. "Maybe there's something broken in the soundbox. There's a little latch under here—"

He reached in and groped around in the heart of

the guitar. "There doesn't seem to be anything wrong in here—uh—" he reached a little deeper in—"oh, here's the trouble! There's a piece of something wedged in here that's been ruining the sound. Wonder why O'Hare didn't take it out before he gave me the guitar?"

Larry drew forth a folded piece of paper and closed the latch on the guitar. He strummed the guitar once again, and this time the sound was quite satisfactory. Then, remembering the piece of paper he had taken out, he put down the guitar and unfolded the grimy sheet.

He stared at it. It was a letter, written painstakingly in O'Hare's flourishing script. Larry read it through twice without saying a word, and looked at it a third time almost uncomprehending.

"Why—I don't believe it," Larry said. He held the paper out and scanned it once again.

"What does it say, Larry?" Harl asked softly.

"Yeah. Why the mystery?" Heitor put in.

"I'm sorry. Here—I'll read it out loud. 'Dear Larry,' it says. 'I hope you won't hold it against O'Hare for what he's done. Maybe they haven't missed me yet, but pretty soon they'll find out I'm gone. And you can show them this, after I'm gone.

"'I've switched sides, lad. I want you to tell that to Reinhardt and anyone else who's interested. That was my whole idea in coming along on this voyage. I saw from the beginning that it was what I've always wanted to do. I've decided to join the revolutionaries on Alpha C and help them in their fight for independence.'"

Larry paused and tried to piece together the fragments of his world. Harl was staring solemnly at him; even Heitor was frozen and grim.

65

" 'I know how you feel about all this,' " Larry continued reading. " 'You probably think I'm a traitor to Earth, a rebel and all the rest, and you're wondering how your pal O'Hare could have done it. Well, if the word pleases you, call me a rebel. I'm only doing what I have to do. Someday you'll learn that everyone has to do what he has to do, and that day you'll wake up.'

"What does he mean by that?" Larry asked.

"Finish reading," Harl said.

" 'O'Hares have always been—well, rebels, and I can't let my father down any more than you can. I can't accept any hard and fast rules when I can see better things beyond. The Clan O'Hare is moving to the stars for good. I won't be coming back to Earth.

" 'Don't be angry with me, lad. We all do what we have to do, and this I must do. Just as you must go to space and serve the Patrol. Have a long and great career, Larry, and keep that guitar well tuned. Your friend always, Patrick O'Hare.' "

Larry put down the letter.

"I never dreamed he'd do anything like that."

"I did. He told me about it a long time ago," Harl said. "He was planning to do it all along."

"He never told me," Larry said. "He never told me."

He stood stiffly, looking at the letter, acutely conscious that O'Hare's stunning personal rebellion made an impression on him that not even Browne's impassioned plea for freedom had. He had felt toward O'Hare as he'd felt toward few people before, and here was O'Hare running off to join the rebels too. When he got back to Earth Larry had planned to tell his father all about O'Hare, hoping to get him a promotion of some sort. But he knew now that his father would never have approved of his friendship with O'Hare in the first place. O'Hare was a tubemonkey, not a Patrolman. Just a big ox who cleaned the jets.

And now he would be fighting against Earth. Sudden tears blinded Larry's eyes, and anger filled him and drove all else from his mind. O'Hare couldn't! He couldn't join the rebels! For a moment Larry hated the big fellow for running away to London Colony. He was destroying everything Larry held most dear. He had no right to—

Suddenly Larry was conscious of his two roommates standing silently and staring at him. They didn't understand, he thought. No one did. But maybe there was still time. Maybe.

He moved abruptly to the door.

CHAPTER 10

W HERE ARE you going?" Harl asked.

"To tell Reinhardt. He'll be able to keep O'Hare from getting a copter, if he's not gone yet."

Harl moved between Larry and the door. "You mean you'd report O'Hare to the captain? He's your own friend!"

Larry looked at Harl. The short, squat Martian had the door blocked. Heitor circled uncertainly somewhere behind.

"Get out of my way, Harl."

Harl made no move. Larry stepped forward and tried to push him, but he was firmly planted and Larry could not budge him.

"You're a traitor too!" Larry said. He could hardly see from rage; somewhere in the back of his mind he knew that he was hopelessly ensnarled in something he did not understand, but now all he was conscious of was that he had to get through that door.

He grabbed Harl by the arm and tried to twist him away from the door. The Martian was barely five-six, and Larry was an even six feet tall, but Larry knew Harl outweighed him considerably and his muscles, trained under the rigorous gravity of Jupiter, would serve him much better on this heavy world than Larry's Earth-trained ones.

Harl gave a little and backed away, taking Larry with him. Larry succeeded in pushing Harl toward the center of the room and tried to break away and dash through the door. But Harl held him fast. Larry tugged but could not break loose.

Harl drew Larry to him the way a fisherman would reel in a fish, and held him. Larry managed to work one arm loose from Harl's grip and push away with it, levering off Harl's chest. He widened the gap between them and with a sudden twist got his other arm loose. They circled each other, breathing hard, Larry trying to break past Harl to the door and Harl waging a defensive fight to keep Larry in the room.

Larry looked at his short adversary. Harl's dark-skinned face was set in an iron mask of concentration. Time was on his side, and he only had to keep Larry under control. Larry felt all of his anger and frustration rush to the surface. Harl, his adversary in argument all through the voyage, had now become his physical adversary as well.

Larry dashed at Harl as hard as he could, hitting him amidships with his shoulder. A bolt of pain shot down Larry's arm, and Harl went spinning across the room to crash against the wall. He hit hard and stayed there a moment, and Larry rushed to the door, only to find Heitor standing by the door with a confused expression on his face, as if he did not know whose side to take in the struggle. Larry shoved him aside and, just as Harl recovered himself and headed for him, he opened the door.

He dashed through, Harl following and grasping for his arm. Larry raced out the door and collided with someone who was coming in. For a moment he thought he would ignore the collision and keep going, but then he realized who it was he had crashed into.

Captain Reinhardt.

Immediately the mad dash ended. He stood as straight as he could and tried to catch his breath. The captain stared at him gravely. There was a long silence.

"May I ask what's been happening here?" the captain said.

Larry said nothing. Harl said nothing. Heitor said nothing. The three cadets looked at each other and at the captain. There was another long silence.

"I—"

But just as Larry began to speak, there was the sound of a copter taking off just outside. Captain Reinhardt strode to the window and watched as the copter rose over the wall and headed out toward the jungle.

"What was that?" he said.

"O'Hare, sir," Larry said. "He's going to London Colony to join the revolution!"

"What!"

Larry nodded. Harl abruptly left the room without a word.

"What was that fight about?" the captain snapped.

"It was unimportant, sir. Just a squabble. But O'Hare left this note for me. Said he's decided to join the rebels."

"I see," the captain said. "When did he leave the note?"

"Just now."

"And why didn't you come to me immediately, Cadet Stark?"

Larry paused. He didn't want to incriminate Harl, but there was no other explanation. And Larry was beginning to feel that Harl had even less love for Earth than he thought.

"Because—because Cadet Ellison delayed me, sir," Larry finally said, feeling like a betrayer.

The door flew open and Olcott burst into the room.

"O'Hare, sir! He just grabbed a copter and took off in it!"

"I know," Captain Reinhardt said. "You say he's joined the rebels, Cadet Stark?"

"Yes, sir. And when I went to tell you Harl—I mean —well, we got into this fight, sir. When you found us."

"What sort of fight?"

"A meaningless one, sir. It was just an argument that turned into a brawl."

"Where is he now?"

Larry looked around. "He's—that is, he was a minute ago—I was sure—"

"He just walked out, sir," Heitor said.

"Go find him," the captain said. "This is serious."

There was a roar from overhead. They all turned to look out the window.

Another copter was soaring over the wall, heading for the jungle.

"I don't think we'll find him now, sir," Larry said.

CHAPTER 11

Is HE a traitor too?" the captain asked. "Is there one loyal man left in my crew?"

Larry felt sick. First O'Hare, then Harl.

"Let me get this straight," Captain Reinhardt said. "O'Hare took a copter to go to London Colony. He let you know first. You were on your way to tell me when you got into a fight with Cadet Ellison. Now he has taken a copter too, presumably to go to London Colony also. Right?"

Larry nodded.

"I think it's time we cracked down on this. You two—Stark and Van Haaren—get a copter and go to London Colony too. Tell them you're switching sides too; tell them anything. But find out exactly what they plan to do, when they plan to go up in arms, and get back here as soon as you have something concrete. Then we call in the Patrol and let them squash this. Tell those two turncoats that they're under arrest as deserters. Olcott, give these cadets a copter."

Olcott led them downstairs and let them have one of the copters parked in the street. It was an old model, Larry could see, probably some twenty or thirty years old. He knew no jetcopters were being manufactured on Alpha C IV, and wondered how much else of Centauran life depended on imports from Earth.

They climbed in. Despite the age of the copter, it was equipped with standard controls and presented no problems. Larry swung into the pilot's seat and Heitor sat next to him.

He checked the compass and got the engine working, and they felt the copter lift. London Colony was a thousand miles due west; the planners of the colonies had established their settlements according to a neat geometric pattern.

The copter cleared the wall, crossed the clearing, and headed out over the jungle between the two colonies.

As Larry looked down through the front window he saw wingfingers hovering over the green, strange-looking trees just a few dozen feet below. Farther down, on the ground, he caught glimpses of the great beasts of the jungle, roaming in search of food, locked in combat, paddling around in the many lakes and streams.

Uneasily he lifted the copter another fifty feet. He had no wish to be any closer to the turbulent jungle below.

"What happens when we get there?" Heitor asked.

"I'm not at all sure," Larry admitted. "We'll snoop

around a little and head back. Maybe we can get those two to come back with us."

"Some chance," Heitor snorted.

The copter roared on over the jungle. Larry watched the fuel indicator with some alarm; it showed the tank was almost empty. They had left in such haste that he had forgotten to check it.

The compass showed them traveling in the right direction. Larry stepped up his speed; if the fuel was going to give out, he would just as soon have it give out someplace else than in the heart of the jungle.

An hour passed. Larry stared impassively ahead, watching for some sign of London Colony, while Heitor remained silent. Larry tried to forget all about the events of the past day and concentrate solely on piloting the copter.

The fuel-tank indicator finally reached zero. Larry knew he had a little fuel left anyway, a safety reserve, but it would not be enough to get them to London Colony. He squinted out over the jungle.

"Look," he said, nudging Heitor out of his reverie.

They looked. Far off in the distance they saw the wildness of the jungle begin to thin out into a clearing, and then they saw a great wall standing high and separating the colony from the wilderness.

For a wild moment he thought he had gone in a circle and arrived back at Chicago Colony, but the village he could see was much bigger than the other colony, and the compass confirmed that he was at London Colony—almost.

Heitor suddenly noticed the fuel-tank indicator for the first time. Larry had carefully not said anything about it to him, reasoning that it wouldn't do any good to have both of them worrying.

"I know," Larry said. "We may make it or we may not, depending on the size of the safety margin in this copter."

But he knew they would not. The engine was starting to sputter already, and they would never make it to the colony, which was at least ten miles off.

They traveled on for a minute more in silence and then the motor began to choke in earnest.

"This is it," Larry said. "We're going to come down here—and we'll have to leg it through the jungle for the rest of the way."

The copter began to slip lazily down to the jungle. They were about a mile from the wall, Larry noted. He guided the copter down through the trees as best as he could. It hit the ground gently and they leaped out.

Larry consulted his compass and they headed off toward the west. Five thousand two hundred eighty feet, Larry thought. One mile through this prehistoric jungle. He took a couple of steps. Five thousand two hundred seventy-five feet, he thought.

He headed through the jungle, warily, with Heitor behind. The jungle smell was overpowering—humid, tropical, overwhelmingly alive and growing. It was dark down under the trees, and the vegetation was twisted and tangled and they were hard put to make much headway through the thick plant life. They marched as quickly as they could, not looking anywhere but straight ahead. Larry tried hard not to think of the dinosaurs roaming through the jungle.

The jungle was alive with sounds—the chittering of a billion insects, the curious croak of the wingfingers soaring overhead, the thumping of froglike animals in the streams, and, someplace off in the distance, the great booming roar of some huge reptile.

The direct nuisance of the insects bothered Larry more than the distant menace of dinosaurs. They walked through what amounted to a soup of insects of all sizes which flew at them, covered their faces with little bites, got in their eyes and ears. Occasionally an immense dragonfly the size of a turkey would buzz by, droning an ominous note.

Larry set as fast a pace as he could, and Heitor puffed along behind. They had traveled for ten or fifteen minutes—Larry estimated another five minutes would get them out of the jungle and into the clearing —when Heitor sank down on a rotting tree stump.

"Wait a minute, Larry," he called. "I'm winded."

Larry turned and saw Heitor wiping the sweat from his face. He was exhausted, Larry saw, and there would be nothing he could do to get him to move.

"Come on, Heitor," he said impatiently. "Just another few minutes and you can rest inside the walls." He batted away a large insect which came too close. "Let's go."

Heitor continued to mop away perspiration. "I can't, Larry. I'm not as strong as you are."

"But we're exposing ourselves to all sorts of dangers as long as we're in the jungle, Heitor. Come on—I'll go slowly so you can keep up."

"O.K., Larry," Heitor said. A smile crossed his pudgy face. "Why not catch a dinosaur and I could ride on him?"

Just then a small animal bounded out of the thick vegetation behind them, gave them a puzzled glance, and continued at a rapid clip. It was some three or four feet high, standing upright like a kangaroo on two legs, balancing on a long tail, and holding two tiny arms folded at its chest.

"There's one now," Heitor said. "A small one. I

76

don't think he could carry me." Heitor struggled to his feet. "Well, let's get on. But slowly."

They moved onward at a reduced pace for a few minutes more. An immense butterfly whose beautifully colored wings were the size of serving dishes flew by. Two more of the small kangaroolike animals came by, moving with great speed, and a third somewhat larger followed them. Two more of a different sort, but still small, followed.

A wingfinger trumpeted overhead. Larry stepped up the pace, sensing something unusual happening in the forest, and Heitor, panting, tried to keep up.

They heard a great crashing off to the left. Larry looked through the trees and dimly saw one of the ponderous twotails crashing through the forest in a path parallel to theirs. Browne had said they were harmless, but Larry was uneasy about the nearness of the great beast. It might not eat the two cadets, but in its clumsy way it might trample them if their paths coincided. Larry watched it, and saw with relief that it was wending its way toward some body of water hidden behind the trees.

A small brown and green animal skittered out from under their feet and climbed the trunk of a scaly tree right in front of them. Larry chuckled with amusement at the little squirrel-like beast, but the amusement turned to horror as he saw what he thought had been a vine suddenly come to life and wind itself around the little animal.

He turned to show it to Heitor. But Heitor was sitting again, wiping the moisture from his cheeks.

"Up, Heitor. Come on. Look—that light ahead is the clearing."

It was another five hundred feet or so to safety, he estimated. They had just about done the impossible by traveling for a mile through the jungle without accident. Larry was not going to risk it now. He pulled Heitor to his feet.

"Just another few steps, Heitor."

"I can't, Larry. Just let me sit here." The insects and the heat and the mile hike had combined to leave him almost exhausted.

Larry saw there was no use dragging him. He would give him a minute or two to rest and then they would continue.

The sounds of the jungle seemed to be getting more intense. The great deep roaring of the dinosaur somewhere in the heart of the jungle—did it seem nearer? Larry decided it was just his imagination.

Two more small reptiles rushed past them from behind. Why were they running only in that direction? he wondered. Was there something behind them?

"Let's go, Heitor. Up, boy." He was going to say something else, but it was drowned by a sudden great snarl.

The trees behind them began to whip wildly about, and the snarl grew to a bellow that filled the jungle. Larry looked up and saw a giant reptile standing over them, roaring as it advanced through the jungle. In the split second before he could move, he saw that it was at least a hundred feet high and all teeth. Then he began to run, shouting wildly for Heitor to follow him.

CHAPTER 12

THE ROAR of the dinosaur seemed to fill the jungle. Larry felt oddly calm as he ran. It was only five hundred feet to the clearing, and just a hundred yards or so from there to the protecting wall. And it seemed too much like a dream for him to feel really afraid.

Once he looked back. Heitor was chugging along a few feet behind him, his face contorted with exertion. And behind them, trampling everything in its way, came the dinosaur. Its head was high in the trees, and Larry suspected it was not hunting them in particular but just out on a foraging expedition looking for some succulent titbit as a snack.

Heitor slipped and fell. Larry reached out and

caught his arm and dragged him along till he clawed his way back to his feet.

"Go ahead," Heitor gasped. "Go on—run!"

Larry said nothing, but continued to pull Heitor onward. The dinosaur had paused to investigate something hiding in a treetop.

A hanging vine whipped around Larry's face. He disentangled himself, kept running, and burst into the clearing. The wall of London Colony rose high into the air a hundred yards away.

Larry heard Heitor's frantic panting not too far behind, and knew that Heitor had managed to get out of the jungle on his own power. The earth seemed to shake under the pounding of the dinosaur's tread as it, too, emerged from the jungle.

Larry reached the gate of the wall breathless and looked back for Heitor.

The other cadet had fallen from exhaustion and was sprawled out on the ground. The dinosaur had paused and was looking down at him with curiosity.

For a second Larry thought of dashing out, grabbing Heitor, and dashing back, but he let that thought drop. Heitor was at least a hundred feet away, and the dinosaur would simply snatch up both of them. No; some less foolhardy plan would be necessary to save Heitor.

The huge reptile was bending over Heitor now and poking him tentatively with the tiny kangaroolike arms which it used as hands. It squinted its great saucer of an eye in an attempt to get a better view of the strange-looking creature on the ground in front of it.

Apparently it had not made up its mind what to do about Heitor, Larry saw. Heitor was still alive and making feeble attempts to crawl away, but he was overcome with exhaustion and seemingly paralyzed with fright.

Larry saw one way to save Heitor. He picked up the largest rock he could see, danced out to within ten feet of the great beast, and hurled the rock at the dinosaur's face.

The 'saur emitted a tentative growl, as if it were not suite sure it had been hit. Larry found another rock and threw it at the dinosaur.

The fact that there was a second creature, this one menacing him, slowly trickled through the dinosaur's tiny brain. Heitor, Larry saw, was reviving and was aware of Larry's strategy, for, while Larry was distracting the animal, Heitor began slowly to crawl toward the gate.

The bewildered dinosaur shook its massive head from side to side as it tried to puzzle out the situation. Larry danced back and forth agilely, throwing stones from different sides of the dinosaur's head. A rock thrown from Larry's left told him that Heitor, who had reached the gate, was adding to the dinosaur's confusion.

Larry saw no further reason to provoke the animal, which would probably solve its dilemma by striking out at anything in its reach, and he ran backward till he reached the gate. The dinosaur continued to weave back and forth in indecision, looking now for Heitor, whom he had almost forgotten, and then for Larry. Finally, trumpeting a cry of rage and desperation, he charged at the wall.

Larry and Heitor backed inside the gate, knowing they were now in perfect safety, and watched as the dinosaur crashed into the wall with a mighty impact. It drew back again—neither the dinosaur nor the wall showed any sign of damage—and hit the unyielding wall. It clawed futilely at the wall with its two small forefeet, bellowing its anger against the small animal which had cheated it of its prey. Finally, in pain and outrage, it ceased belaboring the wall and turned and strode off into the jungle.

They turned to enter London Colony, and walked straight into the arms of a group of men in green uniforms, one of whom was Harl.

"Come to visit us?" Harl asked.

Larry stared at him coldly, but then remembered he was planning to pretend to be a turncoat.

"I've come to join the revolution," Larry began, struggling for breath after the escape from the dinosaur. "But we got a pretty unfriendly reception from one of your watchdogs."

"Yes," said a tall man. "We saw the dinosaur come out and that attracted our attention." He turned to Harl. "What do you think, Ellison? You know them."

"I'm inclined to suspect this one," Harl said, pointing to Larry. "He's always been so loyal to Earth."

"And now you want to join us?" said the tall man.

"Yes," Larry said.

"I think he's lying," said a short, rotund colonist. "I think he's a spy!"

"So do I!" someone else shouted.

The tall man, who seemed to be in command, frowned. "Suppose we lock them up for a while," he said. "Then we'll find out whether they're with us or against us."

"Lock 'em up!" the short man said. There was general agreement at this, and the tall colonist nodded and directed the others to take Larry and Heitor inside the colony.

It looked just like Chicago Colony, except for great banners strung in the streets.

FREEDOM FOR ALPHA CENTAURI
NO TAXATION WITHOUT REPRESENTATION
WE DEMAND INDEPENDENCE
SEVER THE BOND WITH EARTH

A green and red flag hung from a flagpole which stood high in the street. The pole was newly cut, Larry noted; the wood was fresh, and he suspected that just a few days before it had been a proud jungle tree.

The flag was dotted with four lightning bolts, apparently the new flag of the colonists.

They bundled the cadets into a car—an old model, Larry noticed again—and drove off to an impressive building located on the other side of the colony, near the great wall. The tall man introduced himself as Carter, head of the provisional government at London Colony.

They mounted the steps of the building, Carter and Harl and a few of the green-uniformed colonists, with Larry and Heitor. "This is the capitol of the Free World of Alpha Centauri IV," Carter announced.

The inside of the building was almost bare.

"Sorry we couldn't furnish it better," Carter said, with a genial smile. "But the previous occupants took most of the decorations with them when they moved to Chicago Colony. Give us time and we'll have it properly fixed up for guests."

He pointed to a staircase, and the cadets descended silently.

"Next floor you'll find your apartments," Carter said.

They went down further. It was dark and damp below.

"Down this corridor, please." Carter led the way and Larry and Heitor followed, with two colonists bringing up the rear. Larry began to curse the whole foolhardy business of going to London Colony.

"I think it would be best to give you chaps private rooms for a while," Carter said. He turned to one of the colonists. "Take this one and put him in Block A." He tossed a key to him.

"Are we going to be locked up indefinitely?" Larry asked.

"Until we've determined your loyalty," Carter said. "You may very well be genuine converts like Ellison. But if you're not, and if you're equal to walking through the jungle to get here, it might be dangerous to let you roam around."

The colonist led Heitor off with him down a winding corridor. Larry heard a cell door creak open, and the colonist said something. He heard Heitor say something in protest, but the echoes distorted it so he couldn't pick out the individual words, and then the cell door closed with a clang.

"Come," said Carter. "Let me show you your room." He led Larry off down another corridor. Larry wondered why he was taking all this so calmly, and realized it was probably because he would be doing the same thing as the colonists if he were in their position. Besides, after the escape from the dinosaur, this imprisonment seemed comparatively unimportant.

"You realize there'll be trouble for you on Earth for this," said Larry.

"I'm hardly in a position to care," said Carter. "In here," he said, opening a cell.

Larry entered.

"Sorry the accommodations aren't all that could be

84

desired," Carter said as Larry sank down on the cell's hard bed. "I hope they'll be temporary."

Larry leaned back on the bed. "All right, Carter. Just lock up and go back upstairs."

Carter laughed, clanged closed the door of the cell, and walked away.

Larry sat quietly in the darkness thinking hard. It was almost a dream. Only a few weeks before he had been a top-ranking cadet at the Space Academy, and now he was caught up in a revolution and imprisoned.

He smiled despite himself. It was hard to believe that this was all really happening. Perhaps he would wake and find himself back at home, instead of in a dank prison on Alpha C IV.

But it was no dream. He thought of Harl, who had given up everything to join the revolution, wearing the green uniform of the revolutionary army instead of the Grays of the Patrol. And O'Hare, too—did they have a uniform here to fit his giant frame?

Suddenly he leaped off the bed and ran to the gate of the cell, trying to peer out through the bars into the darkness. For he could hear, coming toward him in the dark, the steady beat of footsteps.

CHAPTER 13

THE DARKNESS was too thick for Larry to see anything but dim shadows. The footsteps continued until they reached his cell. He heard the tapping of something on the metal of his cell door.

"Larry!" someone whispered.

"I haven't gone anywhere," Larry said.

"It's me—Harl." The other figure lit a match and Larry saw the face of the Martian.

"Hello, turncoat," Larry said.

"I thought we'd been through that before." The match flickered and went out, and once again they were left in darkness. "They sent me down here to talk with you."

"Go ahead," Larry said. "Talk."

"They've decided that you and Heitor are spies. They intend to keep you here."

"Why won't they believe we've honestly changed sides?"

Harl laughed. "Quit it, Larry. They asked me and I told them. I know you're still working for Reinhardt."

A moment passed in silence. Larry stared impassively out into the black, trying to discern Harl's features, and wondering why he was unable to hate Harl the way he knew he should.

"You *are* still on Reinhardt's side, aren't you?" A note of doubt seemed to tinge Harl's voice.

"Yes," Larry said resignedly. "Yes. He sent us here as spies. I suppose there's no point in trying to bluff it any more. I never thought they'd believe us."

"No. We never did."

Larry noted Harl's use of "we." He was fully on the other side, then.

There was silence again, and Larry began to suspect that Harl had vanished into the darkness. But after a moment he spoke again.

"Tell me, Larry: just *why* do you stay loyal to Reinhardt and his bosses? Give me a sincere answer. Have you ever thought it through carefully, or are you just following blindly along because you think it's the right thing?"

"I don't know," Larry said.

"Whereabouts on Earth are you from?" Harl asked.

"Appalachia. New York City, in the State of Appalachia. Western Hemisphere—North America."

"I know," Harl said. "I studied geography. That means you come from what used to be called the United States of America, before the Consolidation."

"That's right," Larry admitted. He stared glumly

ahead; his eyes were getting used to the darkness and he could almost see Harl's face.

"Man, man! You're from America, and this revolution doesn't mean anything to you? How can you be so dense?" Harl's harsh whisper rose to a rasping half-voice sound. "Don't you know how your own country got its start? The very same way the Centaurans are doing it! Tell me: what was the main slogan of the American Revolution?"

Larry thought. It was all so long ago—he had studied it in Medieval History, though.

"No taxation without—without—" He paused as the force of what Harl was saying struck him. "No taxation without representation."

"Exactly!" Harl said triumphantly. "Now where have you seen that slogan anywhere else, Larry? Think hard," he said sarcastically.

"The banners in the streets of London Colony," Larry said in a small voice. "They said the same thing."

Harl chuckled. "So here we are. You now find yourself taking the side of Great Britain against the Americans. Now let's see you justify your refusal to help us. How can you remain loyal in the face of all this?" Harl demanded.

"I don't know," Larry said. He was very confused, and all the arguments he'd had with Harl now seemed to have gone for naught. He had been wrong and Harl had been right, and he should have admitted it long before.

"You don't know," Harl mimicked. "But you still stick with Earth, because it's what your father and grandfather did. Why, you may think you're nineteen or twenty or so, but you're just an old fossil. You're as stodgy as they come!"

"Harl—Harl—how could I help the revolution? What could I do?"

"You don't mean you're considering joining us, do you? What would Commander Stark say if he found out?"

"Just answer me," Larry said quietly. "What could I do—me, in particular—to make it worthwhile giving up Earth?"

"President Carter had a plan all worked out. You could be very useful to us."

"How?" Larry asked. His eyes had now become accustomed to the dark, and he could see Harl's face watching him earnestly.

"We planned to let you go back to Chicago Colony as if we had never caught you and let you sabotage the *Carden's* radio. That way Reinhardt won't be able to get the reinforcements here until we're all set up."

The thought made Larry shudder. Sabotaging a Patrol ship's radio! Suddenly he realized that his conditioning was too deep—that, though he was almost fully sympathetic with the revolution, that he could never force himself to do such an outrage. But he decided not to tell Harl until he had heard the rest.

"Go on," Larry said. "What happens after I smash the radio?"

"Well, once we're safe from armed Patrol forces, we can proceed with our plans. We grab Reinhardt and hold him as a hostage, along with all the other Earthmen and pro-Earth colonists. This gives us a bargaining edge, and we begin setting up our defenses. We build camps in the jungle, fortify them against the animals. In the meantime Centauran agents now on Earth arrive with the warcraft we've been purchasing with our export profits and any other money we could scrape up. We settle down for a lengthy defense of the planet—or, as we hope, Earth won't even bother to go to the expense of sending ships here to get involved in guerrilla warfare, and they'll let us go. But it all depends on whether or not we can get Reinhardt out of the way and his radio silenced."

"I see," Larry said. "That means I'm a key piece in the machine."

"Just about," Harl admitted. "Carter went wild when he heard me say that you were the radio operator. He saw it was our best chance of knocking out that communications set. What do you say?"

"Let me think about it a minute," Larry said. He sat down on the hard bed in one corner of the cell, and tried to balance all the factors.

He knew now that the revolutionaries were more right than wrong, Earth more wrong than right. Neither side was completely right nor completely wrong, but Earth was definitely not being fair. It was hard for him to accept the concept of Earth's being in the wrong, but Harl had driven it home so many times that at last he acknowledged it.

But still—even if the revolutionaries were right, why should he get involved? If he could get out without joining them, he could go on to become an officer in the Patrol—his fondest dream as long as he could remember—and possibly someday have enough influence to help the Centaurans that way. If he joined then now, it would mean giving up the Patrol after years of dreaming and years of hard work, all to be thrown away in a moment. All to live on a wild, primitive planet and fight against Earth.

The revolutionaries were right. But sabotage a Patrol ship's radio to help them? What if the revolution failed and he were brought back to Earth in disgrace, to stand trial in a court which might include his

90

own father? Larry thought of the commander, how at first he would be unable to believe what his son had done and then how he would calmly wipe all memory of Larry from his mind, as if he had never existed.

"No," Larry said.

"Are you sure? Hurry it up—Carter's waiting to get things under way."

"No," he repeated. "I can't do it."

Harl stared silently at him. "I thought you'd finally grown up, Larry. I see you haven't, not really. You can't take the one step more you need to make it."

"I can't give up the Patrol, Harl," Larry said. "And my father—and Earth—it's too much to ask, all at once. Your side is right, but—" His voice trailed off weakly.

"I see," Harl said coldly. "You just can't do it, I'll tell them. All right." He turned to leave and Larry watched him move away.

"Harl?"

Harl stopped and turned back.

"What do you want?"

"How long will they keep us in this prison?"

"They would have let you out now. I have the key with me. But now you'll have to stay here till your trial. I wish you had listened to me, old man; you're not as dense as you try to be."

"Trial?"

"Your spy trial. Caught in enemy territory, remember?"

"But we had our Patrol uniforms on—" Larry objected. "You can't try us as spies if we had our uniforms on."

Harl laughed. "Sorry, Larry, but we're a little too serious about this revolution to worry too much about ancient Earth rules of war. It's harsh, but our lives depend on it. You're a spy."

91

"But the penalty—?"

"If they find you guilty, Larry, the penalty is the same one they have on Earth. Death."

The blackness seemed to close in around Larry.

"Death?"

"You heard me," Harl said. "I'm sorry, but I gave you a chance."

"You could help me escape—you have the key—"

"Don't ask me that," Harl said. "Maybe we were friends once, aboard the *Carden*. But this is war, and I'm on the other side. I can't help you any more; you'll have to help yourself."

Harl turned again and this time kept moving. Larry watched him as long as he could, until Harl disappeared in the dark. Then he looked after him. He saw that Harl was perfectly serious—that their earlier friendship would not stand in the way of the revolution.

CHAPTER 14

LARRY SAT QUIETLY in the darkness for a long while. He was now a martyr for real—he had had a chance to save his life by betraying Earth, and he had refused.

But he didn't feel at all noble. He felt like a fool. Earth had not earned his life.

Once again the feeling that it was all a dream wandered over him. It seemed incredible that he should be sitting in a dungeon somewhere on Alpha Centauri IV, on trial for his life. He reached out to feel the wall of the cell. It was clammy and cold, and very real. This was no dream.

He heard footsteps approaching once again.

"Harl?"

There was no answer. He heard the key turn in the lock, and the gate slowly swung open.

A giant figure stood silently in Larry's cell.

After a moment it spoke, in a deep murmur. "No noise, lad. It's me—O'Hare."

Larry could hardly repress a whoop of joy. "Pat!"

"Right. But sorry circumstances I'm finding you under, lad. Harl's told me you won't be sensible. But I knew from the first you weren't sensible. No sensible person would come back aft to sing songs."

"So Harl's told you everything, eh?"

"Yes. I won't press you any further, Larry. If you want to stay loyal to Earth, I'll not argue. We won't let a difference in politics end our friendship so soon."

"I'm to be tried as a spy," Larry said.

"Oh? I suspected as much. It looks bad, indeed. But you know what Harl said—"

"How'd you get into my cell, Pat?"

"I'm your jailer, Larry. I have your key."

Larry thought for a moment. "O'Hare?"

"Yes, Larry?"

"I want to get back to the *Carden*. Could you—no, I guess you can't."

O'Hare bowed his head; Larry could see the gesture even in the darkness. "I can't do it, Larry. I've switched sides, now. Remember what I wrote you: enemies are friends, friends are enemies. If I let you go back to the *Carden*, it'll be bad for the side I'm on. No, Larry. It wouldn't make sense."

"You're not a sensible man, Pat. You said so just now yourself."

Larry fowned. He hated to be doing this, but his father had often told him that the important thing was to survive.

"Pat—Pat, remember that time outside the ship?"

Larry felt his face grow hot with shame; he was begging for his life now. But he had to get out.

"How could I forget it, lad?"

"Pat—the punishment for spying is death."

O'Hare silently looked at him. Larry saw now that he had O'Hare firmly caught. He wondered what he would do when he got back to the *Carden*—whether he would ever destroy the radio.

"I see," O'Hare said slowly. "I see what you want, and I can't refuse. There are some loyalties higher than political ones, Larry. I can't refuse."

He held open the gate. "Go on—go," he said in a choked voice. "Go before I change my mind. Heitor stays here, though—I don't owe him anything too. If you're lucky enough to get out of the building, you'll find a jetcopter parked in back. Chicago Colony—you know the way. Due east, a thousand miles. Now, go—and good-by, lad."

Larry lingered for just a moment. "Thanks, O'Hare. Thanks—and good-by," he said softly. He went through the open gate and tiptoed down the corridor, looking back just once at O'Hare, who was still standing in front of the empty cell.

He did not feel very heroic about it all.

Getting out of the building seemed to take years. Fortunately Larry remembered the way he had come, so he reversed his field and tiptoed through the winding corridor and up the staircase, up the second flight, and up into the main floor of the building.

A door in the main hall was open, and Larry saw Carter, the head of the revolutionaries, seated at a desk, reading some reports. No one else was in sight.

Larry considered running through the hall and out the open door, but decided against it. Carter would certainly be attracted by a running figure, but he might not even bother to look up at someone merely walking out of the building.

Slowly he walked through the hall, as if he were walking on eggs. He passed Carter's office with his breath drawn in, walking almost on tiptoe, eyes rigidly forward. Carter turned almost automatically to look through the door as Larry passed, and then turned back to his desk, apparently not realizing who it was going by.

Another step, then another, and Larry was through the open door and out into the fresh Centauran air. Alpha Centauri was high and burning yellow; off in the corner of the sky was pale Beta with its ghostly light. Proxima, the third sun in the system, was nowhere to be seen; the tiny red star was probably below the horizon.

Now, to find the copter, Larry thought. O'Hare had said it was parked "in back." Larry trotted quickly around to the back of the administration building, but found an empty lot and nothing more.

He scowled and bit his lip. This was bad. Without a copter, he was as good as in the cell, since he was a thousand miles from help with no means of reaching it. A trek through the jungle was impossible—Larry recalled his earlier jungle experience, and tried to multiply it by a thousand. He thought of the wingfingers hovering overhead, and the great reptiles. He needed a copter.

He looked up. A hundred yards away was the great wall. And—he whistled in amazement—parked atop the wall was a jetcopter.

Larry set out in a sprint for the wall, his boots clattering against the concrete street and sending echoes reverberating through the quiet colony. He arrived at the wall winded and quickly found the steps leading to the top. He paused for breath before beginning the climb, looked around, and saw three figures come running out of the administration building.

The chase was on already. He had less time than he had thought.

Larry climbed the wall in a rush and ran toward the copter. Standing next to it, calmly polishing its propeller, was Jon Browne.

They stared at each other in mutual amazement.

"What are *you* doing up here?" Browne said as Larry approached.

"I could ask the same thing. But never mind that. I need your copter."

Browne looked down to the ground. Larry's eyes followed, and he saw men starting to climb the steps to the top. Not much time left, Larry thought.

"What? Do you think I'm going to let you escape? Let's see what these men have to say about it."

"I want the copter," Larry repeated.

"You can't get away with this," Browne said, determined to stall until the reinforcements arrived.

All's fair in war, Larry thought grimly. He knocked Browne sprawling and leaped into the copter.

It was then that he discovered it was an ancient model and he had no idea how to start it.

He studied the control board for a moment, then pressed a button which seemed to be a starter. The copter gave a little lurch and jumped ten or twelve feet in the air, and hovered directly overhead. Larry looked out and saw three colonists coming up to the top of the wall, and Browne struggling to his feet and pointing.

"No time to waste," he said, and pressed another button. The copter shot away from the wall at a blinding speed, and headed out over the jungle. He looked

back and saw a group of colonists standing on the wall
—he could barely make them out at this distance—and
waving their arms furiously in the air. Larry wondered
how long it would take for them to begin to pursue.

He looked back and saw a pair of copters coming
after him. But he had a considerable head start on
them, and they seemed to be dropping farther behind,
until at last they veered off in another direction and
disappeared. Puzzled, Larry devoted his attention to
his main problem, which was finding Chicago Colony.

A thousand miles due east, O'Hare had said—but
which way was east? He had no compass. He could be
going in any direction at all. He decided the best
plan would be to continue straight ahead.

The copter seemed to fly itself, once it had been put
into motion. It maintained a steady course, almost skim-
ming the tops of the trees, heading straight and fast.

Larry studied the steaming jungle below. It was all
that could be seen. There was no sign of London
Colony behind, nor of Chicago Colony ahead. All
around, front and back, was the jungle.

As the copter rushed by, Larry caught glimpses of
the great beasts living below—living without any sus-
picion that the planet was no longer theirs, that its pos-
session was being contested by two groups of absurd
pygmies from another star.

The wingfingers were abundant over the jungle.
Larry got a good view of one which kept pace with
the copter for a minute or two. It was mostly wing,
with a tiny body surmounted by a long, fierce beak.
The wings were leathery and were stretched batlike on
a framework formed from the greatly extended fingers.

Larry's wingfinger seemed perfectly capable of moving at the great speed of the jetcopter, but after following along for a short time it sheered off and swooped down on the treetops below.

The copter continued its steady course. Time drifted by; Larry almost forget where he was and what was happening, as he watched the monotonous green below. But after a while he noticed a dot of gray up ahead, which grew and grew until he realized it was the great wall which ringed Chicago Colony.

He hovered over the colony for a moment, wondering how to land the copter. There was no apparent landing gear, and he didn't want to risk a belly-landing. Finally he decided to hover over the wall and leave the copter floating in mid-air while he clambered down the rope ladder.

Now he knew he had to get back to the Earthmen quickly. He still was not sure whether he would tell Reinhardt everything that happened or smash the radio after all, but he knew he had to get back. He raced down the steps and toward the first colonist he saw.

He was a dark-skinned man with a beard. Larry ran up to him.

"Can you tell me where the Earthmen are quartered? I think I'm lost."

The colonist spoke in a soft, deep voice with an overtone of puzzlement. "What Earthmen? Are you feeling well, boy?"

Larry stared at the colonist. What he had suspected of being a dream was fast turning into a nightmare.

"The Earthmen from the Spaceship *Carden*, sir. They were living at the Chicago Hotel, but I can't seem to get my bearings."

"You'll have difficulty finding the Chicago Hotel here, young man. This is Bombay Colony."

"But—" Larry stopped, overwhelmed by rage and frustration. He realized what he had done: he had gone the wrong way and landed at Bombay Colony, which was off to the west, instead of at Chicago Colony. No wonder the London Colony copters hadn't bothered to chase him; they saw he was going to get lost.

The problem now was whether Bombay Colony had been alerted for him and would imprison him again.

He noticed the bearded colonist watching him curiously.

"I have to get back to Chicago Colony immediately," Larry said. "I'm lost."

The head of the Bombay Colony was a tall, distinguished man with an unpronounceable name. Larry explained his predicament in as few words as he could, saying nothing about the revolution but simply acting like a frightened cadet who had been joy-riding and had gotten lost. If communications between the colonies were as slow as he hoped, they might help him before they found out he was a fugitive.

The man with the unpronounceable name nodded his head.

"I suppose we can redirect you," he said. "Where did you leave your ship?"

"My ship is hovering over the wall, sir," said Larry. "I couldn't figure out how to land it."

He waved to a young man in a military uniform standing near the door. "Come on, then. We'll have to get it down before a wingfinger flies off with it," he laughed. "Chandra—you'll find a copter hovering over the wall at 140 North Quadrant. That is where you said you came down, isn't it? Give this fellow a compass and point him toward Chicago Colony and let him go."

Larry breathed a sigh of relief. Apparently there would be no trouble here.

"You care to stay here tonight as our guest?" the tall man said.

"No," Larry said nervously. "I'm afraid they will miss me if I stay away too long."

"All right," the tall man said. He nodded dismissal.

He sat in silence until the ship reached Chicago Colony. This time Larry recognized some familiar buildings. He left the copter hovering over the wall again and headed for the hotel, expecting at any minute to be stopped by men who had followed him from London Colony or Bombay Colony or by Chicago Colony revolutionaries. But he walked unopposed and unnoticed through the quiet streets.

Finally he found the Chicago Hotel. He realized for the first time that he had not the slightest idea how much time had elapsed since he had left Chicago Colony. There had been the trek through the jungle, and his stay in the dungeon, and the wrong-way trip to Bombay Colony. It might have been hours or days.

He was bedraggled and exhausted. His once-proud uniform was torn and ragged; his face was grimy and covered with sweat.

He decided the first thing to do was to report to Captain Reinhardt.

CHAPTER 15

THERE WERE RINGS under the captain's eyes; this had been no pleasure jaunt for him. Larry saluted as crisply as he could, but he was unable to conceal his fatigue.

"You're back just in time," the captain said. "Last night's meeting puts us in an awkward position."

Last night's meeting! Then the whole adventure had taken not quite twenty-four hours! Larry tried to arrange the thought to fit his fatigue.

"While you were gone, Chicago Colony voted to join the revolution. Henrikstown came through with a repeat vote. Only Bombay Colony seems to be leaning back to Earth again. But that means we're likely to find ourselves in the midst of a revolution—a shooting one—before long. What did you learn in London Colony?"

Larry made up his mind not to tell of the plan to sabotage the radio.

"It's the center of the revolution," he said. "The leader is a man named Carter. London Colony has already proclaimed itself the capital of the Free World of Alpha C IV," he said. "Carter is the provisional president of the revolutionary government."

There was a knock on the door. President Harrison of the loyalist government entered.

"Do you know a man named Carter?" the captain asked.

"Revolutionary leader at London Colony," Harrison said. "He's the one who started it all. Everyone at London Colony is solidly behind him and favors a revolutionary war if necessary."

"How about the other colonies? Will they fight?"

"Chicago Colony probably will. I'm not sure about Henrikstown; Bombay Colony is divided half and half but is supposedly more pro-Earth than not, and won't revolt. But they'll support London Colony if all the other colonies do."

"Where's van Haaren?" Captain Reinhardt asked.

"We were both captured by the London Colony colonists," Larry said. "I escaped; he's still there. I found a jetcopter and got away, only I went the wrong way and wound up at Bombay Colony. They sent me here."

"What did you find out about London Colony?"

"That they plan to revolt, sir."

The captain scowled. "More definite! When? How? Didn't you find out anything more definite than that?"

Larry felt his face go red.

"This information may be vital to Earth, Cadet Stark. Do you realize that? Now: what did you find out?"

"I can't, sir."

Captain Reinhardt looked at him with eyes burning with anger. "You—*can't?* You can't what? Are you in your right mind, Cadet Stark?"

President Harrison started to say something conciliatory, but the captain ignored it.

"Cadet Stark: I order you to tell me everything you know about this revolution."

Larry faced the captain and gritted his teeth. An order was an order.

"They—they plan to seize all of us—and you—and hold us for hostages, sir."

There; it was out. He had betrayed them all now, Harl and O'Hare and Carter and all the others. He wondered what his father would say of all this: he had been trapped into a maze of lies and counter-lies, of evasions and betrayals and humiliations. He had sold everybody out now, and had nothing to show for it.

"I hoped this would never happen," President Harrison said. "It means a long, bloody struggle, and no one will profit. We could have settled this peacefully."

"Peaceful settlements are temporary ones," Captain Reinhardt said coldly. "There's but one way to end revolutions."

He sat down at a desk and began writing.

"How many people are there at London Colony, President Harrison?" asked Captain Reinhardt, as he wrote.

"Over two thousand, Captain Reinhardt," Harrison said.

"Hmmm. I hope it won't be necessary to wipe them all out," he said. "Excuse me, President Harrison. Come with me, Larry."

"Where to, sir?"

"Back to the ship. President Harrison, will you cir-

104

culate the word that the crew of the *Carden* is to move back aboard ship immediately?"

"Are you leaving then?" he asked.

"Not yet. But I feel we have stayed long enough within the walls."

The crowd was in the streets as the men of the *Carden* moved back to their ship, and they jeered and cursed sullenly as the Earthmen passed through them.

There were banners hung in the streets of Chicago Colony now—the ones Larry had seen at London Colony, and some new ones.

GO HOME, EARTHMEN
WE DON'T WANT YOU HERE!
DOWN WITH HARRISON

Larry feared that the mob might attack them as they went through the streets, but they kept their distance, milling aimlessly about.

It was comforting finally to reach the wall, cross the clearing, and climb the catwalk that lead into the ship. Larry's bunk aboard ship was strangely empty; he thought of Harl, wearing the green uniform of the revolutionaries, and Heitor, languishing somewhere in that dark London Colony prison.

Captain Reinhardt sent for him as soon as they had re-established themselves aboard ship.

"There's a third-order Patrol fleet somewhere in this sector," he said. "I want you to transmit this message to them at once." He handed Larry the sheet of paper he had been writing on earlier.

Larry saluted and headed for the radio room. While the instruments warmed up he read the note.

"Lao-tze Reinhardt to Space Patrol Commander Carr,

emerg X4. Revolution brewing on Alpha C IV; plan to take all Earth supporters hostage. Come with armed force immediately, prepared to quell rebellion. *Suggested punitive measure:* partial or total destruction of London Colony, originator of rebellion."

Larry looked at the message several times. *Suggested punitive measure: partial or total destruction of London Colony.*

Partial or total destruction.

Partial or total destruction.

He could not do it. Calling the Patrol now would mean the death of O'Hare, of Harl, even of poor Heitor who had nothing to do with it. It would mean turning Alpha C IV into another Jupiter—a rebellious colony crushed by the armed might of Earth. Sending the message would end all hopes of liberty for Alpha C.

Automatically his fingers flew over the controls of the machine, setting up contacts, sending the beam out into space, searching for the Patrol fleet.

"Fleet X16532, Centauri Section," came a voice in his ears. *"Who is this, please?"*

Larry stared at the message. *Partial or total destruction.* He started to crumple the sheet, but realized that that was no solution.

"Who is this, please?" the metallic voice repeated. Larry smoothed out the crumpled corner of the message, and looked at the words, in Captain Reinhardt's stiff up and down handwriting, until they ceased to have meaning and became just a collection of individual letters.

He could not do it. He broke the connection in the midst of an exasperated *"Who is this?"* from the fleet operator, and walked out into the corridor.

"Have you transmitted it yet?" said Captain Reinhardt from further up the corridor.

"Not yet, sir," Larry said, controlling his voice. "Mechanical difficulties; it'll take a moment or two to make contact."

"Hurry it up, then. We have to get them here before anything serious starts here."

"Yes, sir."

Larry turned back into the radio room and let the machine warm up again. There was no escaping it: the message would have to be transmitted. But Larry would not let himself be the agent of London Colony's destruction.

"*Fleet X16532,*" the voice said. "*Who is this, please?*"

"Lao-tze Reinhardt to Space Patrol Commander Carr," Larry began in a weak voice.

"*I'll connect you with the commander,*" the fleet operator responded.

Larry stared at the complex machine in front of him. In a moment he would be giving his message to Commander Carr and setting in motion the wheels that would crush Alpha Centauri IV. No. He could not do it.

He opened the door of the radio room and looked out. Coming down the corridor was Paolo Campbell, a tall, gangling cadet he had known vaguely at the Academy and had had next to no contact with on the voyage so far.

"*Commander Carr speaking,*" the radio said. "*Go ahead.*"

"Paolo," Larry whispered.

Paolo kept moving. "Paolo!"

"Eh? What is it, Larry?"

"Come in here, will you?"

Larry looked at the message in his hand.

"*Go ahead, please,*" Commander Carr said. "*We are awaiting your message.*"

"I want you to transmit an order for me, Paolo."

"Why can't you do it? It's your job!"

Is there something wrong with the connection? Do you hear me? Answer, please."

Beads of sweat rolled down Larry's face. If only Captain Reinhardt would not appear and add to the confusion—

"Never mind that. Just do it for me."

"I don't know how to, Larry," Paolo said.

"All you have to do is read it from this slip of paper," Larry said, exasperated. "You can read, can't you?"

"All right, if it's that important. Give me your message."

There was the sound of a click, as Commander Carr broke the connection.

"Just a second. Let me make the connection again."

Larry manipulated the dials. After a moment's silence the fleet operator came on again.

"What's going on, please? Is this a joke?"

"Sit down here," Larry urged, pushing Paolo into the seat. "Just read this."

He handed the paper, now folded and crumpled, to Paolo. As Paolo began to unfold the paper, Larry left the room, unable to listen.

CHAPTER 16

HE PAUSED at the door, turned, and went back in. Paolo was just beginning the message.

"Hold it, Paolo," he said. "I'll do it myself."

Paolo looked around, mystified and angry. "What's going on, Larry? You playing games?"

"Shut up," Larry snapped. "I said I'd send it." He felt clammy with sweat, and knew that Paolo might very well report his puzzling conduct to the captain.

"If you say so," Paolo said. "Feeling all right?"

"Proceed with message," the radio said.

Paolo left. Larry sat down at the radio and stared at the piece of paper.

"Proceed with message. What is going on, please?"

Larry opened his mouth as if to say something, and then let it slowly close. He reached over and turned off

109

the set, interrupting a puzzled protest from the other end. He sat there quietly watching the quiescent radio.

Larry tried to balance everything. The message could not be sent. O'Hare, Harl, Heitor, the whole revolution, against Larry Stark. Larry Stark, he knew, was not big enough to outweigh all the others. The scales tipped relentlessly.

Carefully he ripped Captain Reinhardt's message into halves, then quarters, then eighths, and let the pieces trickle to the floor. He reached inside the cooling set and carefully unclipped the central power tube —the irreplaceable central tube. He looked meditatively at the tube for a moment and put it in his pocket.

Commander Stark would never approve, he thought. But maybe he would. With a quick motion of his hand he reached inside the set and ripped apart the delicate wires which formed its circuits. He surveyed the wreckage for a brief instant, touched the tube in his pocket to make sure it was safe, looked at the fragments of the message on the floor, and left.

"Did you take care of the message?" Captain Reinhardt asked him.

"It's all taken care of," Larry said calmly. He saluted and walked on, down the corridor and out to the catwalk, and down the catwalk to the ground, thinking of his father, of the Patrol, of Earth, of Harl and O'Hare and the revolution, and crossed the clearing and headed for Chicago Colony.

The man he had to find now was Jon Browne.

The hotel seemed as good a place to start as any. When he approached he saw it had been taken over by the revolutionaries and was being used as a headquarters.

"Is Browne here?" he asked a guard at the door. "I have to see him. At once."

"What do you want with him?" the guard said coldly.

"I have to see him," Larry said.

"Suppose he doesn't want to see you?"

"I don't have time to play guessing games," Larry said. He forced his way past the guard and into the hotel. The guard followed, shouting.

"Grab him!"

In an instant he was surrounded by guards, and he was struggling and kicking and fighting to break free.

"What's going on here?" said a new voice. Immediately the struggle ceased. Larry, held by two burly colonists, looked up, and saw Jon Browne standing there.

"Quite a fighter, aren't you?" Browne said. "You're a better fighter than you are a pilot, anyway. I've heard about your trip to Bombay Colony."

"I'm sorry I knocked you down, Browne," Larry said. "I needed your copter."

"I gathered that. What's been happening here?"

"I have to get to London Colony immediately. To warn them. You have to let me go."

"To warn them? I understand you went there once, supposedly to join them. Now you want to go again?"

"I mean it this time," Larry said. "Let me go!" He struggled with his captors and succeeded in freeing one arm.

"Let go of him," Browne said. They did and he moved away from them.

"Now: am I to understand you've changed sides? You're the most changeable young man I've ever encountered. But luckily I have to go to London Colony myself this afternoon, and I suppose I can take a passenger. You can warn them all you like when you get there. Tie him up," he said.

The colonists converged on him again, and this time, without struggling, he let them tie him. He was unceremoniously dumped into the back of a copter; Browne clambered into the pilot's seat, and they took off.

They came down in a great square in the heart of London Colony. Brown got out and waved to someone in the distance. In a moment Carter and a group of green-clad revolutionaries appeared.

"I've brought you back your guest," Browne said. "The one who didn't like your hospitality." He pointed inside the copter.

They let Larry out and untied him.

"How'd you recapture him?"

"We didn't," Browne said. "He walked right into our headquarters, demanding to be brought here. We didn't argue with him."

"If you'd only listen—" Larry began.

O'Hare loomed up in the distance. He blinked in amazement when he saw Larry.

"Put him back in the cell," Carter directed. "We can't put off building the camp any longer."

"You're definitely going ahead with it?" Browne asked.

"Yes," said Carter. "The entire army's leaving London Colony in about half an hour. We'll march till midnight and build the first camp there, and go on to build the second at dawn. We ought to be ready to march on Chicago Colony tomorrow night and grab the Earthmen and then we'll have to make a quick disappearance."

Two soldiers began to lead Larry away. Harl appeared from somewhere and ran along with them.

"What are you doing here?" he asked. "Why'd you come back?"

"If you'd only listen," Larry said. "Reinhardt gave me a message to transmit. He asked the Space Patrol to destroy London Colony as a punitive measure."

"Holy! We've got to tell Carter! He'll have to evacuate immediately."

"No rush," Larry said. "Tell one of these guys to let go of me and I'll show you something interesting."

"Cover him," Harl directed. "Let's see what he has to show us."

The colonists released Larry and drew their guns.

"Don't shoot. Harl, reach into my pocket here—I'm afraid these fellows may get trigger-happy if I do—and take out what you find there."

"Careful, Ellison," said one of the colonists.

Harl gingerly reached into Larry's pocket. His fingers closed on the radio tube and he drew it out.

He rubbed his fingers on it gently. "A radio tube?"

"Yes," Larry said. "The central power tube from the *Carden's* radio."

"The central power tube from the *Carden?*" Harl repeated.

"Yes."

Harl looked at Larry—looked up at his eyes.

"Larry—did you remove this before or after—I mean, was Reinhardt's message ever sent?"

"I never sent it. I pulled the circuits loose and took the tube."

"Larry!"

Carter drew near. "Why isn't he being taken away?" he asked. "Ellison, what's happening?"

"Reinhardt is asking the Patrol to wipe out London

113

Colony. Or—he wanted to ask them. But Stark here sabotaged the radio."

Larry winced. He still could not stand the thought of what he had done.

"Is this true?"

"There's the tube." He reached out and took it back from Harl. "They could fix the circuit, I suppose, but there's no way they could replace this."

"That means—if we march on them now, we'll have them. Do they know what you've done?"

"Not unless they've tried to use the radio since I left. I reported that the message had been taken care of."

"In that case—"

Carter dashed away. Harl pounded Larry on the arm and then followed Carter, leaving Larry alone in the deserted London Colony street as the afternoon shadows began to gather.

CHAPTER 17

LARRY STOOD ALONE in the street amid the lengthening shadows of late afternoon, breathing the air of Alpha C deeply.

He thought of everything he was leaving behind: Earth, his father, the Patrol, everything. He stood there, still, in the quiet street.

Then he remembered Heitor. Was the pudgy little cadet still somewhere in that dungeon? They couldn't leave him behind when they evacuated London Colony.

He had to find that prison building. But all he knew was that it was somewhere near the wall. He began to trot through the empty streets.

After ten minutes' fruitless search he found an old man sitting on a bench, seemingly oblivious to whatever might be happening around him.

He rushed up to him. "Can you tell me where the capitol building is? The one where they have the dungeons?"

"Why are you still here, boy? The others have left."

"Come on, come on, answer me!"

The old man pointed patiently to his left. Larry began to dash frantically, and finally reached the building. He raced up the steps and through the open door.

"Heitor!" he shouted. "*Heitor!*" He rushed to the door that led to the cells. "Heitoooooooor!"

"You don't need to shout, lad," said a quiet voice behind him. "Heitor's not been forgotton. They took him with them."

Larry whirled. "O'Hare!"

"Just locking up, that's all. Carter thought it might be a good idea to protect the capitol building. Let's go outside."

The massive O'Hare led him outside and locked the main door.

"There. Now all's safe."

He turned to go.

"Wait, O'Hare."

"Sorry, Larry. I can't. They expect me up front. I'll see you there."

He ambled down the steps and headed off into the growing dimness of the twilight. A trumpet call sounded in the distance.

Larry watched him go. The trumpet call was repeated, louder.

"Attention. Attention." Carter's voice came over a loudspeaker from somewhere.

"Attention. We are now readying for the evacuation. Listen carefully. At the next trumpet call we are to assemble at the East Gate. Repeat: East Gate. We will

116

proceed in orderly fashion according to the plans previously circulated.

"We will march through the jungle, protected by arms. There will be no danger from the animals, who will run away from our lights. The five hundred people so designated will remain at Camp 1, which is to be established at a distance of twenty miles from London Colony. They will fortify this camp as per plan.

"The remainder will proceed at dawn to Camp 2, which will be located fifty miles from London Colony. Five hundred designated colonists will be left there. The rest will be ferried on to Camp 3, which is ten miles outside Chicago Colony. There they will join with forces from Henrikstown and march on Chicago Colony to seize the Earth spaceship.

"Be ready to move at the next trumpet call."

Night was beginning to fall in earnest now. Larry pondered the events of the past few days. He had been catapulted into a position of great importance to the colonies, and, he felt, he had redeemed himself.

He had redeemed himself, he felt, not only in his own eyes, but in his father's eyes. What was it his father had said so often? "A Space Patrolman must be able to make decisions and keep to them."

He began to walk slowly through the streets.

He came upon a jetcopter parked in the street. He looked at it, and slowly drew the radio tube from his pocket. He reflected that it was still in his power to fly back to Chicago Colony, to the *Carden*, return the tube, and end the revolution before it was really under way.

Larry looked at the tube, smiling, and at the coptor. "A Space Patrolman must be able to make decisions," he said aloud. "And keep them," he added.

He looked up at the sky. The stars were beginning

117

to come through the darkness now, and he stared at them. Alpha Centauri and Beta Centauri had set, of course, but there was still the spectral crimson light of Proxima C staining the streets.

He looked at the stars, knowing that he was giving them up. All his childhood dreams of the Patrol, of racing from star to star, of seeing everything, of being everywhere, were coming to an end. He was giving up Deneb, and Rigel, and Procyon, and the other stars; giving them up for a wild and strange planet.

Somewhere out there, he thought, was Earth—Earth, that planet where he had been born, the planet he had loved, the planet he could never call home again. He tried to find the old familiar Sun and its nine planets, but they were lost among the great sprinkling of stars on the velvet black bowl of the sky.

He could not find the Sun. Perhaps it was just as well, he thought.

The final trumpet call sounded. He looked up at the stars.

"A Space Patrolman must be able to make decisions," he whispered. "And keep them."

Somehow he knew his father would approve after all. For he was being true, not to Earth or the Patrol, but to himself. And that was what really mattered.

He looked at the gleaming little tube he had taken from the radio, and fingered its shining sides. Then he lifted it and dashed it against the ground.

It broke into a million tiny splinters that scattered over the concrete. They gleamed faintly red in the weird light from Proxima Centauri.

He glanced at the wreckage of the tube for a moment, and then broke into a run, running to catch up with the angry, honest men who were beginning the march on Chicago Colony.

118